HIS COUGAR SUBMISSIVE

OWNED BOOK THREE

KL RAMSEY

ROSE

Rose Eklund sat at the end of the large mahogany bar and tossed back her shot of vodka. She usually didn't drink the hard stuff but if she had to celebrate her fiftieth birthday, she'd do it in epic proportions. At least she figured that the hangover she was sure to have tomorrow would be pretty damn epic. She might be another year older but that didn't mean she had to slip into her new year quietly or willingly. She was going to go down fighting and angry as piss about turning a half a century old.

Her son, Corbin, had offered to throw her a party but that was the very last thing she wanted. As far as she was concerned, fifty could come in quietly and no one had to be the wiser. Then, come morning, she was going to march right into her son and his best friend's offices and announce that she was retiring. Sure, it was a little early but why not? Rose had spent her entire life taking care of everyone else and it was time for her to take care of herself for a change.

She had Corbin just shy of her seventeenth birthday and against her parents' wishes. They had begged her to terminate her pregnancy when she found out she was going to have a baby. Her son's father was almost ten years older than she was and when he found out she was expecting, he took off. Her parents had threatened to press charges and throw him in jail for getting a minor pregnant and he didn't bother to stick around to meet his kid.

Rose was forced to grow up quickly out in the world on her own as a single mom. She had a baby who was depending on her and parents who wanted nothing to do with her. She moved into a little efficiency apartment and didn't once allow herself to wallow in self-pity—there just wasn't time for it. She got her GED, finishing up her senior year at night and working at a local convenience store during the day. She relied on the kindness of friends and neighbors to help watch Corbin and after she graduated and could get a better paying job, she decided to pay back the kindness that was shown to her any way she could.

When her ten-year-old son brought home a new friend from school, she instantly took a liking to Aiden Bentley. He was scrawny and shy and for the life of her, Rose couldn't figure out how the two had become friends. Her son was loud and outgoing and usually the biggest kid in his class but he and Aiden seemed to hit it off from the start. Aiden's mother left him when he was little and his father was a drunk who couldn't seem to get his shit together, even for his only son. So, when she saw that Aiden was struggling to get by, she stepped up and lent a hand. Before long, he was spending nights at her house and just about every waking minute too. He had practically moved in with her and Corbin and that was just fine with her. She considered him her son and she could tell he loved her like a mother.

When the boys went away to college, Rose panicked, worrying about what her next stage in life was going to be. She was only thirty-five years old and she wasn't quite sure what she was supposed to do with herself. She took a few college classes and got her AA degree in business management, which came in handy when the guys graduated from college and announced that they were opening their own company. Rose agreed to help out in her spare time and they jokingly called her their assistant. They set up shop in her basement and Rose felt more like a babysitter than an assistant, at first. But the guys seemed to find their niche and grew the small start-up into a multi-million dollar company. She was proud of them and thankful that they kept her around.

She became Aiden's assistant and honestly, that worked for them all. She got to see her two favorite guys and Aiden's kids all she wanted and Rose was sure she couldn't be any happier. But turning fifty had thrown her for a loop and she wasn't sure which end was up. It was time for her to get off the ride and slow down some. She wanted to travel and explore the world while she was still somewhat young and it was about time she took a chance on life. She didn't want to wait another twenty birthdays to find out that she didn't live her life and was too old to do anything about it.

"This one is from the gentleman at the other end of

the bar," the bartender loudly whispered over the bad honky-tonk music. Rose nodded to the handsome man who was facing her at the other end of the bar and swallowed back the shot of vodka, giving him a mock salute when she finished it.

He smiled at her and nodded, sipping his beer. He was probably younger than her, but almost everyone in the bar was except the bartender and he wasn't her type. Rose wasn't much of a dater and the idea of being brazen enough to talk to a stranger at a bar made her nervous. Honestly, she could count on one hand the number of men she had been with since having Corbin and that was fine with her. She had a son to take care of and dating just never seemed a priority. When Corbin was a toddler, her best friend had tried to fix her up with a guy but he wasn't interested in a twenty-year-old with a toddler in tow. Most guys weren't into single mothers at that age and Rose decided to save herself some heartache and time by deciding to stay out of the dating pool. Sure, she was lonely, but she had Corbin and Aiden and a whole drawer full of vibrators.

"Hi," a sexy, deep voice whispered into her ear. Rose turned to find the man who was formerly sitting at the end of the bar, now perched on the seat next to her. "I'm Clayton Nash," he said, holding his hand out for her to shake. "But everyone calls me Clay."

"Um," she stuttered, cursing herself for having the fourth shot. She knew her limit was three but when he sent her the drink, she didn't want to seem rude and refuse. "Rose," she said, placing her hand in his and gently shaking it.

"Nice to meet you, Rose," he said. She couldn't stop staring at him. He was younger than she was and probably the most handsome man she had seen in some time. Honestly, he looked more like one of her son's friends than someone who'd be buying her drinks at a bar. His dirty blond hair was pushed back as if he had been wearing a hat and had taken it off and his blue eyes matched the plaid blue shirt he was wearing. He reminded her of one of those cowboys she had seen in a western movie.

"Tell me you can ride a horse," she whispered. Rose wasn't sure she had even said those words out loud until he threw his head back and laughed at her. She smiled back but was internally kicking herself for saying something so stupid.

"I can, in fact, ride a horse," he said. "It's kind of a prerequisite for owning a ranch." Rose nearly swallowed her tongue thinking about him fulfilling her dirty cowboy fantasies that she loved so much. They were honestly her favorite romance books to read—the ones with the sexy cowboys but meeting one in real life wasn't something she planned on.

"So what is a beautiful woman like you doing in a bar like this?" he asked.

Now it was Roses turn to laugh. "That is the cheesiest pick-up line ever invented," she giggled.

"Well, I don't know about that," he drawled. "I got to see that pretty smile of yours now, didn't I?" Rose wasn't sure if she successfully rolled her eyes, but she knew she was trying to.

"I'm here drowning my sorrows," she said.

"Please don't tell me that I'm going to have to find and beat the shit out of some asshole for breaking your heart, Rose," Clayton said.

"Oh God, no," Rose almost yelled. "No, no man or boyfriend to speak of," she said, holding up her hand and pointing to her empty ring finger. "It's my birthday," she said.

"Really?" Clay asked.

"Yep, and not a good one at that," she added. Rose sipped the water the bartender handed her and she nodded her thanks.

"What happened to make your day such a bad one?" Clay asked.

"I turned fifty," she admitted with a grimace.

"No fucking way," he said. Clay sounded almost as upset about her age as she felt.

"Fucking way," she said.

"Well, if it makes you feel any better, you don't look it," he said. As sweet as it was of him to say, it didn't make her feel any better. Rose knew that she didn't look fifty and had good genes and night cream to thank for that but she also didn't need anyone to blow smoke up her ass. She knew how old she was and there was nothing she could do about it.

"Thanks," she dryly said. "But it doesn't soften the blow of that number."

"I get it," Clay said. "I'm here for the same reason."

"You're turning fifty today?" Rose questioned.

"Close—forty," Clay said.

Rose groaned and called the bartender back over.

"I'll take a Moscow Mule and another beer for my ancient friend here," she teased.

"Hey," Clay complained.

"How about you come talk to me in another ten years and then you can properly complain about my slight," Rose teased.

"How about we help each other forget that we're turning another year older, Rose?" Clayton asked. Rose wasn't sure if the sexy stranger was asking her what she thought he was but she sure wanted to find out.

"Um, what?" she asked. Clayton smiled up at her and from the devilish grin he gave her, she was sure she had heard him correctly. The question was, would she be a coward and bail or finally do something she wanted and take him up on his offer?

CLAYTON

Clay had a shit day and since it was also his fortieth birthday, his obvious choice for ending his day was at his favorite bar. But tonight, instead of finding all the same prospects, he was happy to find a sexy little blond in a business suit that made him completely hot and bothered. She was wearing sexy high heels that made him want to wrap her long legs around his neck and make her scream out his name. Even her name was pretty and Clay was sure that spending a night over or under her, for that matter, would help him forget about turning forty.

There was no other way he would forget about his milestone birthday. His brother and business partner, Tyler, gave him a good deal of shit about being older and now that he was forty, his brother's propensity for making fun of him only seemed to grow. Of course, it didn't help that his brother was younger than him by eight years. He was still a baby and Clay hated that he was starting to have trouble keeping up with him

8

around their ranch. He didn't dare bitch about his back hurting or any of his new aches and pains otherwise, Ty would never let him live it down.

Now, he was sitting at his favorite bar in town, trying to forget the shit day he had by asking a pretty woman to spend the night with him. Sure, he was probably losing his mind and maybe even his grip on reality, but if he was going down, he wanted it to be with the sexy blond who looked as though she could give just as good as she got.

"So, how about it, Rose?" he whispered close to her ear. He liked the way she shivered as his warm breath brushed over her skin. God, her skin looked soft. "Want to come home with me?" He asked. Rose gasped and turned an adorable shade of pink, making him chuckle. It was refreshing to meet a woman who seemed a little put-off by such an offer. Most of the women he met were usually pasted up against him by this point of the conversation and it was nice to know that women like Rose still existed.

"I appreciate your offer," she stammered. "But I don't think that would be a good idea. I'm a little older than you and we both know that come morning, you'll sober up and forget that you even met me tonight." She was wrong. Clay was only on his second beer and he was about ready to call it a night when he spotted Rose across the bar. Honestly, she looked about as sad and depressed as he felt and there would be no way he'd forget her.

"I hate to break it to you, but this here," he said, holding up his glass, "is my second beer. I'm not drunk,

although I'd give my left nut to be. I'm alone and cele-
brating a milestone birthday, just like you. I thought we
could commiserate together. And I can assure you,
Honey, there would be no fucking way I'd be able to
forget you, drunk or not," he admitted. Rose turned that
adorable shade of red again and he was sure that he was
going to be in a perpetual hard state if he didn't get her
to agree to go back to his ranch with him.

"So, why are you here alone tonight?" Rose asked,
not so subtly changing the subject. Clay could tell that
she had a little more to drink than he had but he was
hoping that the waiter would bring her more water and
less of those Moscow Mules she was drinking. If he was
going to convince her to go home with him, he wanted
her to be sober or as close to it as possible.

"I didn't want to celebrate my birthday with anyone,"
he admitted. "I've never been one for big celebrations or
blowing out candles to mark another passing year, so
here I am." He held his arms wide as if trying to prove
his point.

"What about your wife or girlfriend?" she pried.

He laughed, "Subtle," he teased. "Like you, I don't
have either of those. I have a thirteen-year-old daughter
but she is conveniently on vacation with her mother
right now."

"That's awful," Rose said. "Your ex took her on vacation during your birthday?"

"Yep," he said. "It's fine really. What thirteen-year-
old girl wants to hang out with her father for his
fortieth birthday? My younger brother, Ty, offered to
hang out with me tonight but there was no way I

wanted to spend my night hearing about how old I am from my thirty-two-year-old little brother."

"No," Rose agreed, sipping her water. "I think that would be an awful way to spend your birthday."

"Well, I can think of at least one way I'd like to spend both of our birthdays, but you would have to say yes," he said. He knew he was pushing a little and hell, maybe Rose thought he was a total creep but he didn't care. He wanted a chance with her and if he had to beg for it that is exactly what he was going to do.

Rose sighed and he braced himself to be let down. "I want to," she admitted, surprising the hell out of him.

"Really?" Clay knew he sounded surprised but Rose had caught him off guard.

"Really," she confirmed. "But I have a list," she said.

"A list?" he questioned. "What kind of list are we talking here, Rose?" Clay asked. "Grocery, laundry, chores, demands?" He chuckled at his joke but Rose seemed to find him a lot less funny.

"No, smart ass. A list of things I want and don't want in a man," she said.

Clay whistled his surprise, "So, it is a list of demands then," he said. "I'm guessing it's a long one?"

Rose rolled her eyes and nodded. "According to my son and well, his best friend, I'm a very picky dater. If you could call being out on five dates in the last thirty-three years dating at all."

Clay choked on his beer and set his bottle back on the bar. "You have only been out on five dates in thirty-three years? Shit, Rose," he said.

"Yeah," she whispered. "So, thanks for the offer but I

understand if you'd like to take it back now." Clay knew he had to play the rest of his hand smart otherwise he was going to spend his evening alone and the thought of having to watch Rose walk out of that bar and his life stung a little.

"What's number one?" he asked.

"Sorry," she said, seeming confused by his question.

"The first thing on your list of what you want and don't want in a man?" Clay asked. He knew he might be asking for trouble but he had to know. "If you're going to flat out reject me, I'd like to know the reason why."

"Um," Rose squeaked, "number one would be the guy had to be older than me," she said. Her frown said it all and he knew that arguing would get him nowhere.

Clayton stood and laid down cash for both of their drinks. He nodded at Rose, "Thanks for your honesty," he said, tipping his hat to her. "At least you gave me that. Happy birthday, Rose." Clay turned to walk away and he was just about to the door when he felt a hand on his shoulder. He turned to find Rose looking up at him and the pleading look in her eyes nearly did him in. The country music was so loud that there would be no way he'd be able to hear anything she had to say. He could see her lips moving but that was about it. He pointed to his ear and shook his head as if trying to signal to her that he couldn't hear her.

Clay could see her sigh even though he couldn't hear it. Rose went up on her tiptoes and wrapped her arms around his shoulders, taking him completely by surprise and gently brushed her lips against his. He wasn't sure if Rose was agreeing to everything that he wanted or just telling him goodbye, but either way, he was going to take full advantage of having her pressed up against his body. Clay wrapped his arms around her and pulled her in closer loving the way she seemed to fit up against him and deepened their kiss. When she finally pulled free from him, she was panting and he could tell that he left her just as needy as she did him.

Rose smiled up at him and nodded and he was almost afraid to hope that she was giving her agreement for him to take her home. She didn't give him much time to think about anything, taking his hand into hers and yanking him along to the door. He followed her because honestly, the thought of going home alone sucked. If Rose was offering to spend their birthdays together, he'd make it one neither of them would ever forget—he deserved at least one happy fucking birthday.

ROSE

"Um, so where are you taking me?" Rose asked. He had convinced her to leave her car at the bar and let him drive her home. He was sober and she was—well, less than sober. Hell, she was full-on drunk but still had enough of her good sense to know that agreeing to Clay's private birthday celebration might have been the worst mistake she'd ever made. This wasn't who she was but God, she wanted to be this woman for just one night. Rose was always so sure and steady. It made her a good mom and a good office assistant but she wanted more. She turned fifty and was sure that she was too old to try new things but her old, boring ways were making her feel stale and lacking. Meeting a stranger, albeit—sexy as hell and a cowboy to boot—and agreeing to go back to his place, wasn't on her playlist.

"Well," he said clearing his throat, "we can go to my place if you'd like." She wasn't sure that was such a good idea. "Or," he said when she didn't immediately accept his plan. "We can get a hotel room."

Rose tried to think past the muddled confusion clouding her brain. It would be silly for them to get a hotel room. Plus, Corbin and Aiden had a lot of friends around town and having her son or his best friend find out that she was spending the night with a stranger wasn't something she wanted.

"Your place is fine," she said. "If that's what you would like." Clay took her hand into his own and pulled hers up to his lips, gently kissing her knuckles.

"You always this compliant, Rose?" he asked.

"No," she breathed. Every mile that passed she sobered just a little more and instead of finding this whole idea to be a really bad one, she only wanted it more.

"You don't have to do anything you don't want to, Honey," he said. "If you've changed your mind—"

"No," she almost shouted. "I want this."

"You sure you haven't had too much to drink?" he questioned.

"Oh, I've had way too much to drink," she said. "But, I'm sobering up. I want this, Clay. It's about time I do something for myself, list be damned."

Clay chuckled. "About this list, Rose," he started. "You want to tell me just what I'm up against. I mean, what if my age isn't the only thing playing against me here?" She knew he was teasing but she was sure he was right. If she told him her list, there would be quite a few "drawbacks" to dating him. But, that wasn't what this was. They weren't dating. Hell, they were just having sex and that was number five on her list—no one nightstands.

"Come on, Rose," he pushed. "It can't be that bad."

"It's not good," she admitted. "I made the list when my son was born and I started to think about dating again."

"How old is your son?" he asked.

"Almost thirty-three," she said, cringing at the realization that Corbin was only seven years younger than Clay. But he didn't even seem to blink at his and her son's age difference.

"Well, I know that number one is the guy has to be older than you. We're kind of blowing rule one out of the water tonight. What's number two?" Clay asked.

Rose squinched up her nose and took a deep breath. "No tattoos," she said.

Clay barked out his laugh and she instantly knew that rule number two was also blown to hell. "How many do you have?" she almost whispered.

"A full sleeve on my left arm and one that covers most of my right side and shoulder," he admitted. "That okay?"

"I guess," she grumbled. "As you said, we've already blown past rule one." Clay laughed again and kissed her hand.

"Rule number three," he said. "Let's have it."

"The guy has to have a job," she said. Rose closed her eyes as if silently praying that he wouldn't tell her that rule number three was a no go too.

"Well, today is your lucky day, Rose. I do have a job. In fact, I own a ranch—well, co-own with my brother Tyler. But, you already knew that." Rose thought back to their conversation at the bar, her brain still a little foggy. Yeah, he had mentioned something about owning a ranch when she made a big deal about him looking like a cowboy.

"So, rule number three is safe," she mumbled. "Rule four is probably safe too," she admitted. "I like for the guy to be taller than me. I'm about five-eleven," she admitted.

"Yep, rule four is safe," he agreed. "I'm six-three."

"Wow," she breathed. "That's pretty impressive." Rose tried not to think about what else might be impressive about the sexy cowboy sitting next to her.

"Thanks, but I had nothing to do with that. Just the luck of good genes and all. Rule Five?" he asked

"Rule five is a doozy," she admitted. "We haven't broken it yet, but we are about to."

"I'm almost afraid to ask," he said.

"No one night stands," she dramatically whispered.

Clay glanced over at her and smiled. "Here's your chance to save rule number five, Rose," he offered. "Just tell me no and I'll take you home." Rose wasn't about to tell him no. The longer they drove, the more deter-mined she was to have this whole thing happen between them. She wanted it all—one night of kinky sex. At least, she was hoping that was what she was getting herself into.

"How kinky do you like things?" she asked, ignoring his offer to back out of their deal. "Sex wise I mean." Clay choked and she worried that she had overstepped. "Never mind," she said. "Pretend I didn't ask."

"Well, that's going to be a pretty tough question to ignore, Rose," he said. "Honestly, I like things kinky—

sex-wise," he said, giving her back her words. "Is that okay with you?"

Rose smiled over at him and nodded. "I've always liked kink, not that I've had a whole lot of sexual partners," she admitted. Rose wanted to put her entire fist into her mouth to shut herself up. What was it about Clay that made her want to share her entire life's story with him?

"How many partners have you had, Rose?" Clay asked.

"Um—two," she said.

"I'm not sure if you're asking or telling me," he teased.

"Telling," Rose said firmly, nodding her head for good measure. "Two, definitely two. My son's father and then one other guy before him. We were in high school together," she admitted.

Clay pulled his pick-up onto the side of a gravel road, out in the middle of nowhere and she worried that he was going to tell her to get out of his truck and walk the hell home. "You mean to tell me that you haven't had sex since you had your son?"

Rose didn't look at him, too embarrassed by that truth. She shook her head, looking out the passenger window into the darkness. "And, your son is almost thirty-three years old," he added. God, when he said it like that, she sounded as pathetic as she currently felt.

"Right," she said, clearing her throat. "I was kind of busy raising my son and his best friend when he needed a place to stay after his mom died. When you're busy raising two boys, there isn't much time to go out and have sex," she defended.

"Thirty-three years though, Rose," he said. "That's a damn long time." He didn't need to tell her how long it had been since she was with a man. There were some nights that her whole body ached to be touched, loved, even held. But, there was no one.

"I had my vibrator and my imagination," she said. Clay chuckled and she tried to open her door. "Please unlock my door," she said. "I'd like to get out."

"No," he breathed. "If you don't want this, I'll take you home but you can't get out here. We're in the middle of nowhere. I should know, it's my ranch. You'll be attacked by a coyote or worse if you try to find your way back to town from here in the dark."

"I'll take my chances," she said. Rose fought to keep her tears at bay, not wanting to sit next to a stranger and cry. "I won't let you judge me for my past decisions, Clay." She couldn't stop the sob that bubbled up from her chest and she hid her face in her hands and cried.

"Oh, now Rose, don't do that," he begged. "I'm sorry, Honey. You're right—I have no right to judge you." Clay unbuckled her seatbelt and pulled her across the seat onto his lap. Rose didn't fight him, just cuddled into his chest and God, he felt right. "If I'm being completely honest here, Baby," he said. "I think it's kind of hot that you haven't been with a man for so long. I'm just worried that I might be the wrong kind of man for you," he said.

Rose wasn't sure if she heard him correctly. She sniffled and wiped her eyes, knowing that she probably had smeared her makeup and looked like a hot mess. "Why aren't you the right man for me?" she stuttered.

"Because I'm a demanding asshole, Rose," he admitted. "I wasn't lying when I told you I like kink. Hell, I like a whole lot of kink—I'm a Dom," he said. Rose knew exactly what a Dom was. She had overheard her daughter-in-law, Ava and Aiden's wife, Zara talking about her son and Aiden being Doms. They even talked about a BDSM club that they all liked to go to. She wasn't blind or stupid—Rose knew exactly who her son and Aiden were but that was their lives and she tried to keep her nose out of their sex lives. Plus, what mother wanted to hear about her grown son having sex or what he liked in bed. Still, Rose would often think about what that lifestyle would entail and even had fantasies of someday trying some of the stuff she had looked up online.

"I've Googled some BDSM stuff," she admitted.

"Googled?" Clay asked. "As in you researched it online?"

"Yes," she said.

"And, what did you think?" he asked.

"I think I'd like to try some of the things I saw," she admitted. Clay slid her back over to her seat and reached across her body, buckling her back in. Rose thought for sure that she had said the wrong thing and he was taking her home.

"Hold that thought, Baby," he ordered. They drove the rest of the gravel path back to his house in silence. Rose watched as he quickly put the truck in park, jumped out and rounded his pick-up to open her door.

"Ready?" he asked, holding his arms up to her.

"For?" she questioned.

"For me to show you a few of the things you looked up online. Let me introduce you to my world, Rose," he offered. Rose didn't hesitate; she let him wrap his arms around her body and practically carried her into his home.

"And, about your list Rose," he breathed.

"What about it," she asked.

"I'm about to give you a whole new list, Honey," he whispered in her ear. Rose shivered, causing him to laugh. "Now you're getting the idea, Baby."

CLAYTON

Clay carried Rose up to his master bedroom and laid her across the bed. What he wanted to do was take her down to his playroom and show her exactly what he was about but he didn't want to scare her away. He wanted his night with her and then, if she agreed to be his submissive, he'd introduce her to all his kinks.

Rose sat up on the bed and watched him. He could tell that she was waiting for him to tell her what to do next and God, he loved that.

"You ready for this?" he asked. Rose sat forward and he couldn't help himself he had to touch her. Clay ran his hand down her cheek, cupping her jaw. When he ran his thumb over her bottom lip, her tongue darted out and he couldn't help his groan. All Clay could think about was how her tongue would feel against his cock, just before she sucked him into her mouth.

"Yes," she agreed. "I'm ready. I'm just a little out of practice—as you well know. I need you to tell me what to do next. It's like riding a bike, right?" she teased.

Clay laughed, "God, I hope not," he said. "How about we take this slowly—you know one step at a time. You don't like something, just say so."

"Will I need a safe word?" she asked. "I um, well, I Googled that."

Clay smiled down at her, "Do you want a safe word, Rose? I won't push you too hard tonight but if it would make you feel better, we can come up with one."

"Oh," she breathed. Rose sounded a little disappointed and he worried that he had said something wrong.

"Tell me why you're frowning, Honey," he demanded.

"Well, I was hoping to be pushed a little," she admitted. "Actually, a lot. I wanted you to show me what I've been missing. I won't break, Clay."

"Okay," he said. "Tell me what you'd like to try and we can go from there."

"Um, everything," she said, sitting up on the edge of the bed. "Do you like to spank women?" she asked. He sat down next to her and pulled her onto his lap. He suspected that telling her, "Fuck yes," as his answer might scare her off.

"Yeah," he said, shrugging, going for casual. Rose smiled and nodded.

"I'd like to try spanking," she admitted.

"Do you want me to use my hand, flogger, paddle—" Rose reached up and covered his mouth with her hand.

"Yes," she said. "All of them." Clay like where this discussion was heading. It was giving him the in he was looking for with Rose.

"Well,. If you want to try all of them, we will need more than just one night. You up for that, Rose?" he asked.

"You mean you want to see me past tonight?" she questioned.

"Yeah," Clay admitted. "I do. Are you okay with that?"

"I—I think so," she said. "If you're all right with that."

"We'll need rules," Clay said. "You okay with replacing your rules about who you'll date with new ones?"

"What are we talking here, Clay?" she asked.

"Nothing out of the ordinary. You'll agree to be my sub and I will give you rules that you will need to follow or you'll be punished." Rose tried to scramble off his lap and he banded his arms around her waist. "Just give me a chance to explain before you run off," he said.

Rose stilled on his lap and his cock wanted to complain. "Fine," she said. "What do you mean by having to punish me?" she asked.

"Oh, you know—waterboarding, bamboo shoots up your fingernails, electric shock therapy. I'm sure you saw all of that in your Google search, right?" Clay teased. "What?" Rose questioned. She started to squirm around on his lap again and his cock sprang to life.

Clay chuckled, "I'm teasing, Rose. Punishment can be whatever you agree to. I like to spank with a paddle when my sub doesn't follow the rules."

"Have you had many submissives?" she asked.

"A few," Clay admitted. "I'm a member of a local BDSM club and I like to go there to play. My ex wasn't into the lifestyle and when I admitted that I wanted to try adding some kink into our sex life, she started losing interest. Honestly, it was the beginning of the end, looking back."

"I'm sorry," Rose offered. "If I agree to be your submissive, will you still go to the club to play with other subs?" There was no way he'd want another woman if Rose agreed to be his.

"No," he breathed. "I'm a one-woman kind of guy. But, I'd like to take you to the club to play." Rose smiled up at him and shyly nodded her agreement.

"So, rule number one," he said. "You agree to be my submissive and we both agree to an exclusive arrangement."

"I agree to rule number one," she said. "Is it that easy or will I need to sign something?"

Clay laughed. "No, I don't think we'll need a formal contract," he said.

"How many rules will there be?" Rose asked. "You know I like rules."

"Yeah," he breathed. "But, your rules were limiting you, holding you back. My rules are supposed to free you; help you to experience something new and exciting. You think you can handle that?"

"Yes," she said without hesitation. "I think I might like that."

"Good, Baby," he said. Rose squinched up her nose and he thought it had to be the cutest thing he'd ever seen. "Why the face?" he asked.

"Well, you keep calling me, 'baby,'" she said.

"You don't like nicknames?" he questioned.

Rose shook her head, "I like them but it seems funny for you to call me that since I'm a full ten years older than you."

"I don't give a fuck about our ages, Rose," he growled. "When we're here, just the two of us, you are mine and I'll call you whatever I'd like. I use 'baby' as a term of endearment and that has nothing to do with our ages—got it?"

"Yes," she said. "So, rule number two is fuck our ages?"

Clay barked out his laugh, "Yep," he agreed. "Rule number two is that there is no age difference between us and I'll call you, 'baby', 'honey' or anything else I'd like to."

"I think I'm going to like rule number two most of all," Rose said.

"You haven't heard rule number three yet," he teased. Clay rolled her under his body and kissed his way down the column of her neck.

"What's rule three?" she squeaked.

"Number three is that you are mine—body, mind, and soul. You will do what I want when I want," he growled against her neck. Clay unbuttoned her white silky blouse and let it slide across her body, leaving Rose in just her lacy bra. God, she was sexy as fuck. Rose had no idea just how much she turned him on but she was about to find out. The rest of the rules were going to have to wait because he needed to make her his.

"What about the rest of the rules?" she stuttered as he sucked her nipple into his mouth through the lace of her bra. He gently bit down and she yelped, writhing against his body. He could feel the heat of her core through her sensible business skirt. He had to admit, the whole hot businesswoman thing did it for him. Clay grabbed a handful of her hair and gave it a sharp tug, causing Rose to hiss out her breath. Yeah, she liked a little bit of pain with her pleasure. Training Rose was going to be a whole lot of fucking fun.

"We can finish going over the rules later," he said. "Right now, you should choose a safe word."

"I thought you said I won't need one for tonight," she whispered.

"Plans changed," he murmured against her skin. "I'm going to give you a little taste of what I plan on doing with you and you might need to use your safe word if it gets to be too much."

"O-Oh," she stuttered when he bit into her flesh. He waited for Rose to give him her word and when she smiled down at him and said the word, "Walrus," he couldn't help but laugh.

"Walrus?" he asked.

Rose looked up at him and batted her eyelashes, gifting him with her sexy smile. "Well, I read online that I should choose a word that I wouldn't use during sex. I would not use the word 'walrus' during sex," she defended.

"Fair enough, Baby," he said. "Walrus it is. If you don't like something I'm doing, I want you to tell me. If you want me to stop, use your safe word. Got it?"

"Got it," she breathed. "What will you do with me, Clay?" she asked.

"Sir," he corrected. "When we're together like this, you call me 'Sir.'"

"Sir," Rose purred, rubbing her body against his.

"Thank you, Honey. I'm going to spank your ass red and then I plan on spending the rest of the night making you mine. Spend the night with me, Rose?" he asked. Clay didn't want to sound like he was giving her an order when he asked her to spend the night with him. He needed for that to be something that Rose wanted to give him.

"Yes," she whispered. "I'd like that." Clay let out his pent up breath and she wrapped her arms around his neck. "Thank you for asking, Sir."

"Up," he ordered, helping Rose from his bed. "Strip for me, Honey." She looked shyly down her body and back up at him. Clay sat back and waited her out, watching the indecision cross her features. This was the moment he had been waiting for—the moment she would have to decide what she wanted from him. He just hoped that she would decide that she wanted what he was asking for because letting sexy, little Rose go now wouldn't be easy.

ROSE

"What's it going to be, Baby?" he asked. He had been waiting her out, watching her and Rose could see the hope in his eyes when he asked her for her decision. Rose reached up and unsnapped her bra and slipped it down her arms, letting it fall to the floor. Clay looked her over and she loved the sexy smirk he wore as he blatantly watched her. Clay nodded to her skirt and she unzipped the back and let it fall to the ground around her ankles. She had already slipped off her heels when they got to his place.

Rose Looked down her body and said a little silent prayer that she was wearing her good lacy panties and was relieved to see that was the case. She had on thigh highs with garters that attached to her pink lacy panties. Rose looked back over to where clay sat on his bed and worried that she had done something wrong. He was so still and quiet, she knew that she must have messed up at some point of her pathetic strip tease.

"I'm sorry," she whispered. Clay stood and pulled her down to his lap.

"What the hell for?" he questioned.

"I've obviously done something to displease you, Clay. You haven't said a word since I started taking my clothes off." Rose looked down her body and back up to him.

"You're fucking perfect, Baby," he praised. "I was quiet because I was afraid that if I said anything, I'd end up swallowing my damn tongue. I especially love these," he said, running his hands down her thigh high stockings. "How about we leave this for now?" Rose shyly nodded her agreement.

"Will you take off your clothes?" she asked. She felt so out of her element with Clay. It had been so long since she had been with a man and Clay seemed to have so much more experience than she had.

"Sure," he agreed. Clay unbuttoned his plaid shirt and tugged it free from his body and she couldn't help but let her eyes greedily roam his torso.

"You work out," she said. God, it sounded more like she was accusing him of something rather than praising him.

"A little," he admitted. "It's mostly from working around here—you know dealing with the ins and outs of the ranch. I build a lot of fences." Clay shrugged and she watched as his muscles bunched and moved. He was beautiful. Clay helped her to sit down on the bed next to him and stood to shuck out of his jeans. He stood in front of her in just his boxer briefs, making her mouth water with what she hoped would be next. His erection practically jutted out at her and she wanted to reach for his cock but he hadn't given her permission yet. Rose knew enough about a Dom/sub relationship to know that she had to wait for him to give her the order to touch him. She ran her hands up and down her thighs, eager to have him give the order.

"You want something, Honey?" he asked. She knew he was taunting her; testing her but she looked up at him and smiled.

"I do," she said, nodding. "Please."

"Please what, Honey?" he questioned. Clay seemed to know exactly what she was asking for but he wasn't going to make any of this easy on her. Rose felt tongue tied and saying the words, "I want to give you a blow job," seemed foreign to her. It wasn't something she had ever felt comfortable doing, being forward when it came to sex. Maybe that's why she sat on the sidelines for so long, coming up with one excuse after another to avoid the male population.

"How about I give you time to think about what you want. How about a distraction?" he asked. Rose shyly nodded and he chuckled. Clay sat down next to her on the bed and he pulled her across his lap, his erection jutting into her belly. Rose looked down at the floor and closed her eyes when he ran his big hand over her silky panties. He cupped a handful of her ass and squeezed and Rose just about wanted to run and hide. She wasn't used to anyone paying her ass so much attention.

"How does this make you feel, Honey?" he asked, running his hand over her other cheek and down her thigh.

"Um," Rose squeaked. "Embarrassed." She sounded more like she was asking a question rather than telling Clay how his touching her ass made her feel. Clay gave her ass a sharp swat and it felt like fire had spread from the top of her thigh, where he had spanked her, up her cheek. Clay rubbed the spot where he had landed the first blow and the sharp, hot pain turned to intense pleasure. Rose moaned and writhed against his hand.

"You like that, Baby?" he asked.

"Yes," she hissed. "More, please."

"More please, Sir," he corrected, gifting her other ass cheek with the same attention. She ground her drenched pussy against his thigh and Clay swatted her ass again.

"Hold still, Honey," he ordered. "The more you move, the longer it's going to take me to give you what you want. What do you want, Rose?" he asked. Again, she didn't answer. If she had, she would have told him that she wanted him to help her find her release. Her entire body was screaming for it but asking for something so intimate, so personal, felt wrong.

"You don't like to talk dirty, do you, Rose?" he asked. She kept her eyes trained on the floor, trying not to think about her ass perched in the air, waiting for his attention. He saw her at her most vulnerable. She was completely out of her element, giving him complete control of her body and Rose wasn't sure she liked it. Sure, it was nice not to have to make any decisions but Clay was a stranger to her and letting go and giving him her complete submission wasn't an easy task for her.

"No," she said. "I don't like to talk about sex—you know ask for what I want."

"Did you ever like to talk about what you wanted sexually," he asked. "You know, with your son's father?"

"No," she said. "He was older than I was and I was just a young girl. I didn't know anything about sex back then."

"Oh Rose," he said. Clay helped her to sit up and she was horrified that her admission had him changing his mind about having sex with her tonight. Rose quickly scurried off his lap and covered herself with the blanket he had tossed over the foot of the bed.

"It's okay, Clay," she whispered. "I get it if you're not interested anymore. I'm not what you were expecting. Heck, I'm not what I was expecting either. I guess the alcohol was making me braver than I really am and now —well, I'm just pathetic." She stood to find her clothes. Rose would call an Uber and head back to the bar to pick up her car and try to put this whole horrific birthday behind her.

"Stop," Clay ordered. "Come here, Rose." She wasn't sure why, but she did as he commanded, standing in front of him, almost naked. He took her hand into his and led it to his bulging erection. She playfully let her fingers trace it's impressive outline through his boxer briefs and loved the breathy little groans she elicited from him.

"That feels so good, Honey," he hissed. "Does it feel like I don't want you?" he challenged.

"N-no," she stuttered. Clay held her hand in his, not letting her take her fingers from his cock. "Don't stop," he commanded. Rose felt a surge of courage that gave her the confidence to dip her hands into his briefs and let them freely roam his cock. Clay moaned and threw his head back. It was the hottest thing Rose had ever been a part of.

"Was this what you wanted to ask me, Rose?" he asked. "Did you want to touch me?"

"Yes," she admitted. "I wanted to touch you and taste you, Clay. I still do." That was possibly the dirtiest thing Rose had ever said out loud and a part of her wanted to run and hide.

"I want that too, Rose," Clay said. He laid back on the bed, letting her have full access to his body. "Do whatever you want to me, Baby," he ordered. Rose shyly smiled down at him and nodded. Her tongue darted out and she licked her lips. "Fuck, that's hot, Honey," he said. Rose loved the way Clay challenged her, talking dirty to her like it was nothing. This world was so new to her but Rose was sure she was going to like it.

She leaned over his body and licked his cock from base to tip, cupping his balls with her hand. He moaned and thrust himself at her, as if he needed more from her greedy mouth. "You like that?" she questioned.

"I fucking love it, Baby. More," he ordered. "I need more, Rose. Suck me into your mouth." Rose was not very experienced with blow jobs. Hell, she had only given a few in her lifetime but Clay made her want to try.

She firmly grasped the base of his cock with her hand and wrapped her lips around the tip, letting him push his way into her mouth. "Yes," Clay hissed. "Just relax your throat and let me take over." Rose did just that, loving the way he grabbed her hair to hold her steady. He bobbed in and out of her mouth, hitting the back of her throat and Rose did her best to breathe through her nose. He pushed a few more times to the back of her mouth and tried to pull free from her lips.

"I'm going to come, Rose," he said. That was exactly what she wanted but she wouldn't let him free to give him the words. She sucked him back into her mouth and pressed her fingers into his thighs, holding him in place. "Fuck, Rose," Clay shouted. He pumped in and out of her mouth and before she knew it, he was coming down her throat in hot spurts. She took all of him and licked him clean, pretty proud of her efforts. Rose let him pop free from her mouth and licked her lips.

"Was that okay?" she questioned, suddenly unsure of herself. Clay didn't make a move from the bed, panting as if trying to get air in and out of his lungs.

"Okay?" he asked. "It was fucking perfect," he growled. "Are you okay? Was I too rough with you?"

She smiled down at him, running her fingers over his jawline. He leaned into her caress. "I'm fine," she whispered. "You taste good, Sir." Clay pinned her to the mattress and rolled on top of her.

"Minx," he teased. "Let's see how good you taste," he said. Clay kissed a path down Rose's body, giving her breasts special attention. Her whole body felt as though it was on fire. It consumed her and made her want more. She wanted him to stoke the fires that were always burning in her.

Clay popped her garters loose and made quite a show of working her thigh highs down her legs, kissing and nipping her sensitive skin with each and every inch that he exposed. He finished pulling her panties down her body and settled between her legs.

"You smell good, Honey," he teased. Rose wanted to die from embarrassment but the raw need that consumed her was winning out. Clay didn't give her any time to think or hide. He ran two fingers through her wet folds and she moaned and laid back on the bed.

"Tell me what you want me to do, Rose. Give me the words," he ordered. She sat back up and looked at him like he had lost his mind. Was he really going to make her beg him? Was he going to make her say the words? "Rose," he prompted. "What do you want me to do to your sweet pussy?" he asked.

Rose covered her eyes with both hands, refusing to look at him. "Lick it," her muffled voice commanded.

Clay chuckled and ran the pad of his thumb over her sensitive clit. "Look at me and tell me what you want, Honey," he ordered. Rose knew that disobeying him wouldn't get her what she wanted.

Rose slowly lowered her hands and stared down at him. "Lick it," she squeaked, repeating herself.

"Gladly," he said. Clay smiled and gave her an outrageous wink, making her giggle. Her laughter quickly faded when his tongue slid through her slick pussy.

"Not so funny now, Honey, is it?" Rose lay back again and waited for him to continue. "Rose," he whispered against her pussy. She couldn't help but squirm against his mouth, needing more. "Hold still or I'll tie you down," Clay growled.

Rose tried to hold as still as possible but gave some honest thought about disobeying him. She always wondered what it would feel like to be tied to a man's bed, completely at his mercy, letting him do whatever he pleased with her body.

"You'd like that wouldn't you, Baby?" Clay questioned. He looked up her body, waiting for her answer.

"I'm not sure," She admitted. "I think I might like to be tied up."

Clay smiled up at her. "I think that can be arranged but right now, I'm going to make you scream my name."

"Oh God," Rose moaned. "Yes, please." Clay licked her pussy and she held her breath, trying to hold as still as possible.

"Breathe, Honey," he ordered. Rose let out her pent up breath. She was so close to finding her release and when he sucked her clit into her mouth, she couldn't stay off her orgasm. She shouted out Clay's name and when he finally finished with her, she felt like a lifeless rag doll.

"Thank you," she whispered.

"Don't thank me yet, Honey," he said. "We're not done yet." He drug her limp body to the end of the bed and spread her open. Clay didn't give her a warning; he just sunk into her body, balls deep.

"You feel so fucking good, Baby," he groaned.

Rose reached up and ran her hands down his chiseled chest. "You feel good too, Clay." It had been so long since Rose felt the weight of a man's body against her own or the thrust of a man's cock deep inside of her core. She had forgotten just how good it all felt. Sure, her vibrator was nice but everything Clay was doing to her was a million times better. Rose wasn't sure where she ended and Clay began.

"Tell me you're close," Clay begged. "I am," she said. "I just need—more." Clay seemed to know exactly what she was asking for, snaking a hand between their bodies and rubbing his thumb over her sensitive nub. "Yes," she hissed. Rose rode out her orgasm, taking what she needed from Clay. He quickly followed her over and when he came, he shouted out her name and Rose thought it was the most beautiful thing she had ever heard.

Clay collapsed with her onto the bed and she curled into his body. Rose had never been a very touchy, feely person but snuggling into his body just felt right, especially given what they had just shared.

"You still want me to spend the night," she asked.

"Absolutely," he said. "I can't imagine anyone else I'd rather spend the rest of my birthday with."

Rose smiled and nodded, "Agreed," she breathed. As far as birthdays went, her fiftieth was one for the books and not something she'd be able to forget for a very long time.

CLAYTON

Clay woke up the next morning before the sun and carefully extracted himself from Rose's body to get out of bed. He found his jeans, slipped them on, and decided to start some coffee. It was the only way he was going to get through his morning chores since he had spent most of the night making Rose shout out his name. He turned back to look her over and then made his way to his kitchen.

His house was the original main house for the ranch. The place had been in his family for six generations now and he and his brother, Tyler were the current caretakers of the ranch. Ty lived just down the road in a little house that he, Ty, and their dad built ten years back, just before his dad passed. Now, the ranch depended on the two of them if they were going to pass it on to future generations. Ty didn't have kids yet—or a woman for that matter and Clay had one daughter, Paisley. His thirteen-year-old daughter seemed to have no desire to run the ranch. She spent as little time as possible helping out around the homestead since he and her mother, Abilene divorced. They split up when Paisley was just little and they had been divorced for five years now. His daughter still came to spend weekends with him but she was spending less time out at the barn and refused to do anything around the ranch, including riding her favorite horse—unicorn. Their only hope for passing down the ranch was falling on his brother's shoulders and that had him worried. Tyler was too busy playing the field and reliving his glory days as a quarterback on the high school football team to find a nice woman and settle down. They were fucked but Clay would worry about all that another day.

Now, he had bigger things to worry about—namely the sexy blond who spent the night with him last night. He needed to figure out how to convince Rose that what they did last night wasn't a mistake. Clay was pretty sure that would be her argument when she woke up this morning, given her lengthy list of whom she should and shouldn't date. Her ridiculous list read more like a ransom note rather than a list of what she wanted in a man. Who the hell made lists like that? He had a feeling that once Rose woke up and overthought their night together, she would be rushing out of his house and his life. His only saving grace was that Rose left her car back at the bar and she'd need for him to take her back to pick it up. That would buy him some time so he could figure out a way to convince Rose to see him again tonight.

"Hey," Ty said, walking in through the back door.

"What are you doing here?" Clay whispered.

Ty walked over to the cabinet where Clay kept the coffee mugs and helped himself. "I'm out of coffee and I need my fix," Tyler grumbled. "What's got your panties in a bunch this morning?" Clay looked him over and frowned. "You look like shit, by the way."

Clay took his brother's mug of coffee from him after he got done pouring it. He took a sip of the coffee and scowled. "Thanks for that," he whispered.

"Want to tell me why you're whispering?" Ty asked. "You sick or something?" Clay wasn't sure how he wanted to answer his brother. He thought about lying and telling him he was sick. Maybe that would get him the day off and he could persuade Rose to spend the day in bed with him. But, that wouldn't be fair to his brother. Especially today when they were mending fence. It was a grueling job and he'd be pissed if Ty bailed on him.

"If you have to know," Clay started. Ty's attention was quickly turned by Rose walking into the kitchen, yawning and stretching, wearing just his plaid shirt from the night before. "Shit," Clay cursed.

"Oh my God," Rose shouted. She tried to cover herself with her arms and watching her flail around was almost comical. Clay set his coffee mug on the kitchen counter and crossed the room to stand in front of Rose.

"Morning, Baby," he said, pulling her up his body to kiss her. Rose protested and slapped at his chest until he finally put her down.

"Clay," she breathed. "You could have warned me that you had company."

Clay chuckled, "He's not company, Honey. He's my

little brother, Tyler. Ty, this is Rose." His brother crossed the room to offer Rose his hand. She quickly reached around Clay's body and shook Ty's offered hand.

"Nice to meet you, Tyler," Rose said.

"You too, Rose. I didn't know my brother was entertaining. I'm sorry to barge in on you so early."

"It's fine. I should be going anyway," Rose said. She turned to walk back to his bedroom and Clay shouted at her to stop. She did and he followed her into the hallway. It was now or never—he needed her to give him some promise that their one night together wasn't going to be their only night.

"I have to take you for your car," he reminded.

"No, it's fine, Clay," she said. "I can call an Uber. I don't want to put you out."

He chuckled. Rose was so peculiar and so refreshing from the women that he usually dated or played with at his club. "Not at all," he said. "I insist."

Rose seemed to mull it over and then she smiled up at him and nodded. "I'd appreciate the lift," she said. "It will give me time to get home, grab a quick shower, and head into the office."

Clay worried that he was losing his chance at asking her out again. The thought of what happened between the two of them being only a one-night thing wasn't acceptable to him. "What are your plans for dinner tonight?" he asked. Rose looked at him as if he had lost his mind.

"Dinner," she questioned. "I haven't thought that far ahead yet. Why?"

"Have dinner with me," he said. "Go on a real date with me."

"Last night didn't count as a real date?" she challenged.

"No," he breathed. "Last night was wonderful but hooking up at a bar and bringing you back here doesn't count as a real date. Have dinner with me, Rose?" This time she didn't hesitate or take time to think his proposal over. Rose smiled and nodded her agreement.

"Okay," she agreed. "Will I need to pack my toothbrush or is this offer just for dinner?"

"That depends on what you want, Rose. It's your call," Clay said, although he wanted to tell her to pack more than just her toothbrush.

"I'd like to spend the night again, Clay," Rose whispered. She went up on her tiptoes and gently brushed his lips with hers. Clay needed more and he didn't give a fuck that his brother was standing in his kitchen probably listening to every word they were saying. He pushed Rose up against the hallway wall, pressing her between it and his body. Clay loved the way she wrapped her arms around his neck and moaned into his mouth. When he finally broke the kiss, they were both panting for air.

"That was just a little teaser of what's to come tonight," he said. "I also have a surprise for you and I think you'll like it."

"I'm not much for surprises, Clay," Rose admitted. "But, I'll try to keep an open mind. As long as it's not a surprise birthday party, we'll get along just fine." Clay must have made a face at her mention of a surprise party. It was something he never had and never wanted —a big birthday bash. Honestly, a party like that sounded more like torture than fun.

"Deal," he agreed. "No surprise birthday party for either of us. But, I think you'll like what I have in store for you tonight."

"Mind if I use your bathroom to freshen up?" Rose asked.

"Not at all. You want some coffee?" he asked.

"Please," Rose said. "Cream and sugar if you have it, too," she said.

"Sure. I'll have it ready for you when you're done getting ready," he said. Clay watched Rose walk down the hallway and back to his master suite. He turned to go back into the kitchen and just about ran into his brother.

"Fuck, Ty," he grumbled. "Why are you still here?"

"Well, I thought about heading out to the barn but I wouldn't be able to hear your conversation from there. So, I stuck with eavesdropping from the kitchen," his brother teased.

"You hear enough or do you need for me to recap our private conversation?" Clay spat.

"I got the gist," Tyler said, his stupid smirk in place. "You like this woman, don't you? Usually, you pick a woman up from the club and play with her until you get bored. What's different about this sub?" Clay shot his little brother a look and Tyler shrugged. "I know more than I let on," he admitted. He didn't know Ty was so well versed in the BDSM world. It wasn't something that they discussed but his brother was right, he didn't

44

like to keep a sub for more than a night or two but Rose wasn't just his sub.

"I didn't pick her up at the club," Clay admitted. "I went to Shooters and had a few drinks for my birthday and well, Rose was there drinking for the same reason."

"To celebrate your birthday?" Ty asked.

Clay sighed, "Try to keep up, Ty," he teased. "Rose and I have the same birthday." Clay conveniently left out the part about their age differences because honestly, it didn't matter and it wasn't his brother's business.

"So, you were both sitting at Shooters and commiserating over turning the big four-zero?" Tyler asked.

"Well, one of us was upset about turning forty." Clay chugged down his lukewarm coffee and put his mug in the sink.

Tyler looked him up and down and smiled. "You're baiting me to ask how old Rose is but a true gentleman never asks," Ty said.

"That works for me because a true gentleman doesn't tell a woman's age either," Clay said.

"And," Rose said, standing in the doorway to the kitchen. "A real woman doesn't give a fig about her age because it's just a number. I turned fifty yesterday, Tyler." Clay had to give him credit, his little brother didn't even flinch at Rose's mention of turning fifty. Clay finished making her coffee and handed Rose the mug. She took a sip and hummed her approval.

"Good?" Clay asked.

"Perfect," she agreed. It was strange spending their first morning together with his brother watching on.

45

There were so many things he wanted to ask Rose to get to know her better but having Ty looking on made that nearly impossible.

"I'm going to drive Rose to pick up her car," Clay said.

"That works," Ty agreed. "I'll eat some breakfast and then get started on the fencing. You have any eggs and toast?" Tyler asked.

"Sure, just help yourself why don't you?" Clay grumbled.

"Thanks, man," Ty said. "I appreciate that." Clay shook his head at his brother.

"I just have to run back to the bedroom, grab a shirt and brush my teeth," Clay said to Rose. "You good?" He shot Ty a look telling him to behave himself.

"Yep," she said. "I'll finish my coffee and be ready to go by the time you're done." Clay kissed her cheek and brushed past his brother on his way out of the kitchen.

"Don't worry," Ty said. "I'm sure Rose and I will find something to talk about while you are gone."

"That's exactly what I'm afraid of," Clay admitted and disappeared down the hall. After he had worked so hard to get Rose to agree to another night with him, the last thing he needed was for Tyler to fuck that all up for him. Yeah, he'd just have to hurry and give Ty as little time alone with Rose as humanly possible. That way he'd have less chance to fuck things up with her.

ROSE

Rose played twenty questions with Tyler and she had to admit, she kind of liked the guy. He reminded her a lot of Corbin and Aiden and that thought made her feel ancient. She needed to remember the rules that Clay had set into place for them. Especially the one about age being just a number and not coming into play between the two of them. It was still pretty hard to forget their drastic age difference, no matter how much Clay said it didn't matter to him. Rose just hoped like hell that she'd be able to work past that or this thing with Clay wouldn't work.

The car ride back to Shooters with Clay was about the same as her game of twenty questions with Tyler. He sure did ask a lot of questions but it was nice to have someone take an interest in her that way. When they finally made it back to Shooters, Clay walked her to her car and gave her a scorching kiss in the empty parking lot, promising her that they would pick things up tonight. Clay told her to be ready at six and she promised to text him her home address so he could pick her up. Rose wanted to insist that she just drive over to his place, so she'd have her car in the morning but Clay was hell-bent on picking her up properly for their date. She had to admit, it was nice to be treated like a lady for a change and not like someone's mom, office assistant, or even grandmother, even though she wouldn't trade any of those titles for anything.

By the time Rose showered, changed, and got into the office, she was over thirty minutes late. She stepped off the elevator and almost ran right into Corbin. "Why the fuck are you so late today?" her son questioned.

Rose tried to breeze past him and he stepped in her path. "Corbin James," she chided, knowing how much he hated when she middle named him. "I had something come up and I'm a little late—no big deal." The more she tried to brush off her being late, the more he seemed to press her for answers.

Aiden poked his head out of his office. "What the hell is going on out here?" he asked. "I'm pretty sure they can hear you two arguing down the street."

"Mom was late today and now she's avoiding giving me an answer about why," Corbin said, catching Aiden up.

"There, now you have all the news and we can get on with our day," Rose sassed.

"Mother, you've been acting strangely since last week. I know that turning fifty has hit you hard but you don't have to go through all of this alone," Corbin said. If he only knew how not alone she was while she celebrated her birthday.

"My being late had nothing to do with me turning fifty," she lied. It kind of did since she met Clay while commiserating about turning another year older. Telling her boys about her night with some guy who picked her up at a bar wasn't what she wanted to do this morning.

"Then why were you late, Rose?" Aiden asked. "We just want to make sure that you're all right."

"I'm fine," she said, tossing her bags down onto her desk. "Now, if you both don't mind, I'd like to get on with my day. I have to leave here tonight on time."

"What, why?" Corbin questioned.

"No reason, I just have plans. Geeze son, maybe you should take up a new hobby if you have so much time to wonder what I'm doing with my free time." Rose laughed at her statement. "Maybe take up knitting."

Corbin smirked at her and Aiden barked out his laugh. "I'm going to leave you two to resolve this. I have a meeting in ten minutes," Aiden said. He kissed Rose's cheek. "I hope you had a nice birthday and if you need anything, you know where you can find me."

"Thank you, Aiden," she said. "I did have a nice birthday. I appreciate you keeping your nose out of my business, too." Rose looked at Corbin and he huffed out his breath.

"Subtle, mother," Corbin said. Aiden laughed and walked back into his office, shutting the door behind him. "I stopped by your house last night and you weren't there," he said. Corbin sounded as if he was accusing her of something but she refused to feel guilty about what happened between her and Clay.

Rose turned and stared him down. "I think you are confused about who the parent is here, Son," she said. "While I appreciate you stopping by to visit it doesn't mean I owe you an explanation about why I wasn't home."

"If you wanted to go out for your birthday you could have come over and celebrated with us," Corbin said.

"Again, I appreciate that but I had other plans," Rose said. She was beginning to see that she wasn't going to get away with not spilling the beans about where she spent the night last night. Honestly, she didn't know what she was worried about. She was a grown woman and what she did in her spare time wasn't her son's business.

"The thing is, when I went out on my run this morning, I stopped by your house and you weren't home then either." Corbin crossed his arms over his massive chest and stared her down. Rose almost wanted to laugh at how much he looked like the same angry little boy who used to try the same tactics when he was younger.

"Again, it's none of your business, Corbin. I was out and that's all you need to know." Rose turned back around and busied herself with the pile of folders that Aiden had left on her desk for her. She was hoping that her son would take the hint and get lost but she also knew how stubborn he could be. Corbin was like a dog with a bone when he wanted answers. Rose knew he'd dig down as deep as he could to get to the answers he wanted.

"Were you with someone?" he asked, cutting right to the chase. Rose shot him a look that told him to tread lightly. She was pretty good with her mom faces and if she was doing it right still, she was giving him the, "Don't mess with me" face. "Shit," Corbin grumbled. "You were with someone. You met a man and have been keeping it from me? How long have you been seeing him?"

"It's not like that," Rose admitted. She wanted to cover her face and hide; she was mortified she was going to have to tell him that she picked up a guy at a bar and went home with him. That wasn't the person she was but she wouldn't change a thing about her night with Clay.

"Then tell me what it's like, Mom," he prompted.

Rose sighed, "I met a man last night and well, one thing led to another. The rest is none of—"

Corbin didn't let her finish her sentence. "Yeah, I get it—it's none of my business. But it is, Mom. You're my business and if you're meeting strange men and spending the night with them, I have a right to know."

"You make it sound like I've done this before," Rose whispered. "I don't meet strange men in bars. It was one man and one night."

"In a bar?" Corbin questioned. "You picked up a guy in a bar and stayed with him. Tell me you didn't tell him where you live or give him any personal information about you or our company."

"You make him sound like a corporate spy or something. This man wants nothing to do with your company," Rose said.

"You can't know that, Mom. You don't know him, do you? He could work for a competitor or something."

Corbin paced the floor in front of her like he always did when he was upset or worried.

Rose barked out her laugh. The thought of Clay being out to bring down her son's company was crazy. "I think you're overreacting," she said. "He owns a ranch just outside of town and we were both at the bar for our birthdays."

"You two have the same birthdays?" Corbin asked.

"Yeah," she said. "And we were both miserable about turning another year older. And, I guess I had a little bit too much to drink."

Corbin stopped pacing and looked her over, "Tell me he didn't take advantage of you, Mom," he demanded.

"No, of course not," she said. "He's nice, actually."

"Well, that's terrific," Corbin said. "If he's nice then that's all that matters, right?"

"I was having a shit day, upset overturning fifty and well, he bought me a drink and made me feel special. And, he was just as miserable about turning forty, so we gave each other comfort."

"Okay, first off—eww," Corbin said, squinching up his nose. "Wait—did you say he was upset about turning forty? He's ten years younger than you, Mom?"

Rose looked back down at her desk and nodded. "Yes," she said. "I'm older than him and he's fine with it. Honestly, age is just a number." Rose wished she believed her own words but she didn't. Being with Clay felt right but getting past his first rule of "age doesn't matter," didn't feel like one she'd be able to follow.

"Geeze, Mom," he said. "You get that he's closer to my age than yours?"

"Are you telling me you want to date him?" Rose teased.

"Very funny," Corbin said. "You telling me that's what's going on between the two of you? You're dating now? I thought you said it was just a one-night thing."

"It is—it was," Rose slumped into her chair, suddenly feeling very tired.

"I'm not sure what's going on between Clay and me but I want to find out. He's asked to see me again tonight and I've agreed. I think I like him," she admitted.

"Will I be meeting this younger rancher that you think you like, Mom?" Corbin asked. Rose's first instinct was to tell him no but she also knew Corbin would use his vast resources to figure out who Clay was and go out of his way to meet him.

"At some point," she said. "Let me get my mind around all of this first and then I'm sure I can arrange a meeting."

"What do you know about him, Mom?" Corbin almost whispered.

"I've already told you most of what I know. He's been divorced for five years now and he has a thirteen-year-old daughter. He and his brother, Tyler, run the ranch together. There, now you're all caught up. That's about all I know—unless you want personal details about our activities."

"Fuck no," Corbin growled. "I'd prefer not hearing about my mother's sex life, thank you."

"So, we have a deal then? You let me work out a few things with Clay and when the time's right, you can meet him," Rose promised.

"Yeah," Corbin agreed. "It's a deal. Just take things slow and if you need me, just yell." Rose stood and wrapped her arms around her son's middle. He wrapped her in a bear hug and squeezed her.

"Thanks, Son," she whispered. "Let me go. I can't breathe." Corbin chuckled and released her. "Now, get lost. I have a ton of work to do if I'm going to leave here on time tonight for my big date."

CLAYTON

Clay had spent the day fixing the fencing around the farm. They had a rough winter and now that the weather was breaking, he wanted to get a jump start on patching some of the holes in the fence. His herd would be itching to stretch their legs and allowing them to roam in the southern pasture would be a nice change for his cattle.

He and Tyler had worked opposite ends of the field and that worked for him. Clay knew that his brother probably had a ton of questions about Rose but Clay didn't want to answer any of them. Ty had gotten the gist of what was happening between him and Rose. The rest wasn't any of his brother's business.

"Hey—I just finished up the back corner of the fence. I'm about ready to call it a day, man," Ty said. Clay checked his watch and realized that it was already four in the afternoon. He needed to finish up and get ready for his evening with Rose. He had called and booked a reservation at his favorite restaurant and then, he was hoping Rose would let him take her home. He wanted to show her his playroom and maybe try out some new things with her. What Clay wanted to do was take her by his BDSM club and have some fun with her but they weren't to that point of their relationship yet. She had barely agreed to be his submissive and he wanted to lead her into his lifestyle as easy as possible.

"Yeah, I need to knock off soon myself," Clay admitted. Tyler jumped up onto the back of his pick-up and started unloading the extra posts and equipment that they didn't use.

"You going to see Rose tonight again?" Ty asked.

"If I say yes, are you going to give me a bunch of shit?" Clay questioned.

Ty shrugged and smiled, "Probably," he admitted. "You know that's my job, right? I'm your little brother and it's my duty to give you as much shit as possible, man."

"Well, mission accomplished," Clay said. "You've always been damn good at your job then."

"Thanks," Ty said and chuckled. "Before we call it quits for the day, I do have something I'd like to talk over with you."

"Sure," Clay agreed. "Shoot."

"I'm just spit balling here, but I think I'd like to strike out on my own. Our neighbor is selling off a good chunk of land that butts up to ours. I'd like to buy it and build my own place."

"This is your place," Clay argued. "Grandpa and Dad left the ranch to us."

"I appreciate that, Clay. I really do. But, I also know

that someday Paisley and her family might want to take this over. That's how this generational thing works in ranching. I want to have something to pass on to my kids someday." Ty tossed the last fence post down onto the pile from his pick-up and jumped down.

"So, does that mean that you're planning on having kids then?" Clay teased. He had always hated that Paisley was an only child. He wanted to give her a brother or sister but that was out of the question. He and his ex, Abi had tried for years to get pregnant again but they never did. Abi blamed herself but he insisted on them going to a fertility doctor. That's when he found out that he was the problem. He had a low sperm count and the doctor said he would probably never father any more children. Clay beat himself up for years, even feeling like less of a man. Abi and he grew apart and by the time he picked himself up and put himself back together again, it was too late. Their relationship was over and Abi filed for divorce. He couldn't blame her but it stung like a bitch all the same.

They had lived apart for six months and Clay was miserable. He convinced Abi to give him another chance and that's when he finally admitted that he wanted to try a little kink in the bedroom. He wanted to spice up their sex life. Hell, he wanted complete dominance over her and Abi wanted nothing to do with him. It was the final nail in his coffin and when she left him again, this time, he let her go. It was for the best. She deserved to find someone who wanted the same things she wanted—namely more kids and a vanilla sex life. He also deserved to find someone who might be into the same kinks he was and he had to admit, meeting Rose was a nice surprise.

"I'd like to have kids," Ty admitted. "I'm pretty sure I'll need to find a woman first though."

Clay chuckled and slapped Ty on the back. "Times a wasting," Clay teased. "You might need to leave your house if you plan on finding a willing woman to have your kids, Brother."

"Ha, Ha," Ty dryly snarked. "You think Rose has a younger sister?"

"No," Clay breathed.

"Okay, then how about getting me into your club?" Clay had always suspected that his little brother liked kink but they never really discussed stuff like that. Some things were just off-limits, even with his brother.

"My club?" Clay questioned, playing dumb.

"Sure, that BDSM club you belong to in town. I know you go there, man. I've heard the rumors about what you're into. This is still a small town, you know." Clay knew better than most how small their town was. When he and Abi divorced, he heard nasty rumors flying around that he had cheated on her. Someone had seen him coming out of the club and word got out that he was meeting women there and having sex with them. That part was true but he and Abi had been separated for over a year by the time he first stepped foot in the club.

"I guess I'm just surprised that you're into that kind of thing, Ty," Clay said.

His brother shrugged and gave him a goofy grin. "Yeah well, I don't go around advertising what I like to do behind closed doors. I've always liked a little kink. I just haven't met a woman who was into all of that. Was Abi up for that part of you?"

Clay moaned and hung his head. "You want to get into all of this, man?"

"Sure, Why not? I mean, you are my brother and well, we didn't invent this stuff. I'm sure we're not the first men who liked a little kink, Clay." Ty had a point but discussing his sex life with his little brother wasn't something he thought he'd ever do.

"No, Abi wasn't into what I like. It was just the final straw, you could say. That and my not being able to give her another baby. I guess she just couldn't handle all of it and I can't say that I blame her. We had a lot of good years together and Paisley," Clay said.

Ty smiled, "Yeah, she is a pretty fucking fantastic kid, Clay." His daughter was an awesome person and honestly one of his best friends.

"She is," Clay agreed.

"Does Rose know what you like?" Ty asked.

"Yep." Clay smirked back at his brother. "She seems to be up for all of my kinks and I'm hoping that she'll want to go to the club with me. I'm seeing her tonight for dinner and then I plan on bringing her back to the house and showing her my playroom in the basement."

"Wait, you have a playroom in the basement of the house we grew up in? How the fuck did you manage that?" Ty asked.

"I had it built a little over a year ago. I wasn't sure that I wanted to keep going to the club—privacy issues and all that shit. I had a run-in with a few subs who wanted more than just some playtime and I needed a break from the club." Honestly, Clay was hoping that he would find someone—someone like Rose who wanted to be more than just a fun time at a club. He was looking for a sub and since Rose agreed to be that for him, he was glad that he put that playroom in. Rose was so new to his world she was probably going to need a little coaxing to go to the club with him.

"Lowdown Ranch will never be the same, Clay," Ty teased. "You've taken the place to new levels of class." Clay chuckled at Ty's assessment.

"Shut the fuck up, asshole," Clay grumbled. "You keep giving me shit, I won't get you into my club."

Ty sobered, "Fine—sorry," he said. "So, you'll get me in?"

"Sure," Clay agreed. "But you and I will have to have open communication. I don't need you showing up when I'm there. That would be the last thing I want to see my little brother doing."

"Deal," Ty agreed. "And, thanks, man."

"No problem. Now, I've got to go and get ready for my date. You good with finishing up here?" Clay asked.

"Yep," Ty said. "You go and get all pretty for your date. Have fun." That was exactly what Clay planned on doing with Rose tonight. He planned on having a hell of a lot of fun.

Clay picked Rose up at her townhome and smiled at the crafty way she tried to hide her overnight bag under her jacket. She shyly looked around to make sure that no one saw her as she handed it to Clay and he helped her into the cab of his pick-up truck. He leaned into the cab of his truck and gently kissed her lips.

"Hey," he whispered. "You look beautiful." She did too. Rose wore a black cocktail dress that hugged her every curve and didn't leave too much to the imagination. Her high heels just about made him want to swallow his damn tongue. Clay shut her door and rounded his pick-up to get into the driver's seat.

"Thanks," she said. "You look very handsome too." He had taken time to shower and even get a little dressed up if you could call throwing on a blazer over his white dress shirt and jeans, dressed up.

"Thanks," he said. "I hope you like steak," he said.

"I do," she admitted.

"Great. We're going to a little place in town that I'm part owner of," Clay said.

"You own part of a restaurant?" Rose questioned.

"Yeah," he said. "A few years back my best friend from college asked me for pricing for my cattle. He wanted to source local beef and when I found out he needed a partner, I jumped at the chance. It's one of the businesses I've invested in to help when times are tough around the ranch. We have our good years and our lean years. Having stock in some local area businesses helps me through the lean years."

"I'd love to have dinner at your restaurant, Clay," Rose said.

"Partially own," Clay corrected. "And, thank you,

Honey. I take it from your overnight bag that you will be spending the night with me too."

Rose turned the cutest shade of pink and shyly nodded. "I'd like to if that's still okay," she said.

"It's more than okay," Clay agreed. "I'd like to try a few things—if you're up to it."

"Like what?" Rose asked.

"Well, I'd like to tie you up, if you think it's something you might like." Clay wished they weren't having this conversation while driving. He was hoping to go over all these details at dinner. Instead, he couldn't really gage how Rose felt about what he was suggesting, not able to see her expressions.

"I um, I think I'd like that," Rose stuttered. Clay nodded and pulled into the parking lot to the steak house. He parked around back, turned off his truck and unbuckled her seat belt, pulling her onto his lap.

"This is so much better," he whispered. "I'd like to spank you over my saddle," he said. He didn't mean to just blurt that out, but there it was.

"Over your saddle," she said. "Like out in your barn?"

"No," he said. "I have a saddle in my playroom and God, I'd like to see you sprawled over it while I spank your ass red." Clay ran his hands down over her body to cup her perfect ass. "Would you like that?" he asked squeezing her fleshy globes in his hands.

"Oh," Rose breathed, "I think I would like that, Clay."

"Sir," he corrected.

"I thought I only had to call you that when we are in the bedroom," Rose said.

"When we're together like this you call me Sir and I'll call you mine," Clay growled.

"Yes, Sir," Rose agreed. "What else do you want to do with me tonight?" she asked. A million things ran through his mind and he gave her a wolfish grin. He wanted to do so much with her but he needed to remember that she was new to his world. He was introducing her to his lifestyle and needed to go slowly to let Rose get acclimated to all his needs and desires.

"Well, let's recap," he teased. Clay kissed his way up her neck, over her jawline and when he got to her lips, he paused just a hair from taking them. He liked the way her breath hitched in anticipation and he knew that he had her full attention. "You said you'd like to try being tied up. Is that right?"

"Yes," she breathed.

"And, you seem to like the idea of having me spank your ass while you straddle my riding saddle. Am I correct?"

"Yes," she moaned. Rose wiggled on his lap, doing nothing to help relieve his growing erection. Clay wished he wasn't trapped in his pick-up but he refused to skip any of the date night activities that he had planned for the two of them. Rose deserved a nice night out, a real date, and not just him having his way with her, taking what he needed.

"Rose," he whispered her name against her lips. Clay couldn't help himself; he ran his hand up under her tight skirt and could feel the heat from her core before he even ran his fingers through her drenched folds. "You're wet for me, Honey," he said hoarsely. He wanted to take her right there in the cab of his pick-up but he also knew that there were people in and out of the busy restaurant's parking lot.

"Clay," she whimpered. "Please, Sir."

He wanted desperately to give her what she was begging him for but he also knew that getting caught was too much chance to take with her. "I promise to give you everything you need, as soon as we get back to my ranch," Clay said. "For now," he plunged two fingers deep into her pussy, loving the way her breath hissed from her lips. "I'm going to give you a taste of everything you have to look forward to once I get you back to my playroom."

"Oh God," Rose moaned and threw her head back. "Yes, please." He loved the way she shamelessly rode his busy fingers and when he let the pad of his thumb leisurely stroke over her clit, she just about bucked off his lap. Rose whimpered and rode out her orgasm and when she came, it was his name she whispered on her lips like a prayer. She was beautiful to watch and everything he'd been looking for and God help him—Rose was his. Every minute he spent with her made him more and more aware that Rose Eklund was the woman he'd been searching for. He wouldn't tell her that. Not yet at least. There was no way that he'd want to spook her and give up his chance at showing Rose that they could work together.

Rose slumped against him, breathing hard and flushed from her release. "You are so fucking beautiful, Baby," he praised. Clay righted her skirt and helped her back to her seat. Rose reached for him and he chuckled.

"What about you, Clay?" she protested, running her hands over his erection. "I want to—" Clay covered her mouth with his hand, not letting Rose finish her sentence. If he allowed that, he would take her up on her offer and let her have her way with him. That would lead to him high tailing it out of that fucking parking lot and dragging her back to his ranch and willingly down to his playroom.

"Honey," he said. "I think we need to have a nice dinner and then we can get to the part where I let you do exactly what you want with me." Rose pouted and he chuckled again. "While that's pretty damn adorable, Baby, I want tonight to be perfect. Dinner and then we can play," he ordered.

"Fine," she said, pout still firmly in place. "But you haven't finished telling me what you want to do with me when we get back to your ranch." Clay knew that if he finished telling her what he wanted from her that dinner would be pretty uncomfortable for him to sit through.

"How about we discuss it over steak?" he asked. "I've got a secluded little corner reserved for us and we'll have plenty of privacy to talk the rest of it over."

"All right," she agreed. Clay didn't give her time to change her mind. He got out of his truck and rounded to her side to help her out. She cuddled into his side and he felt like the luckiest man in the world with her on his arm.

ROSE

Rose was shocked at her behavior. Making out in a pick-up truck wasn't something she'd ever thought she'd do. But, there she was, letting Clay give her an incredible orgasm and leaving her carelessly throwing caution to the wind and not caring if anyone saw them. For some reason she couldn't explain, Clay made her want to try new things and be more daring. Maybe it was just time for her to take a chance on life and hope that Clay would want to take a chance on her.

The hostess led them back to a quiet, dark corner in the back of the steakhouse and Rose knew that Clay had arranged for them to have privacy and she had to admit, she liked the idea of having him all to herself. Clay ordered a bottle of wine and some appetizers and she was happy to let him take charge of that for her.

"I hope this is all right," he whispered across the table.

"It's perfect," Rose gushed. "I have to admit that I

usually just go home after work and have a sandwich or a salad for dinner. This is a treat."

"I'm no better," Clay said. "By the time I get done around the ranch, I'm so tired when we knock off for the night that I sometimes don't even eat dinner."

"Well, aren't we a pair?" Rose teased.

"What about your son? Are you very close?" he asked. "If you don't mind me asking personal questions."

Rose giggled and shook her head. "I think we're past the whole no asking personal questions thing, Clay. I mean, you have seen me naked and all." Rose cringed and rolled her eyes.

"Yeah, I guess you're right. I just don't want you to feel like I'm prying," he offered.

"Not at all," Rose said. "We are close. We kind of grew up together. I was just a teenager when I had him and we leaned on each other when things got tough. We have a good relationship. I work for both of my boys."

"Both?" Clay asked. "I thought you said you only have one son."

"Well, that's a long story," Rose said.

Clay held his arms wide, "I'm not going anywhere and I'm pretty sure we can order a second bottle of wine if we need to."

Rose laughed. "All right," she said. "Well, I was raising Corbin on my own. My parents didn't want anything to do with me once I got pregnant and refused to have an abortion."

"What about Corbin's father? Was he in the picture?" Clay asked.

"No," Rose breathed. "He was almost ten years older

than me and well, I was a minor. When I told him I was pregnant, he took off. It didn't help that my parents told him that they would have him arrested if he stuck around. So, he left and I had to make some hard and fast decisions. I decided to raise my son on my own and it was the best choice I've ever made. He became my reason for hanging in there and he kept me going even when I didn't think I could."

"Kids have a way of doing that for us, don't they? Whenever I'm having a bad day, I talk to my daughter, Paisley and it instantly becomes better. She's my reason for being the best person I can be," Clay admitted.

"I always wanted a daughter but I'm afraid I wouldn't know what to do with one, having two boys. When my son brought home his best friend and told me that his mom had just died, it broke my heart. Aiden started staying with us more and more after that. His dad went through a tough time. He lost his wife and was lost trying to figure out how to take care of his son. He started drinking and when he just couldn't take care of Aiden anymore, I took him in and finished raising him." Rose smiled at the memory of Corbin and Aiden being young. It sometimes surprised her that her boys were grown and had kids of their own. It felt like just yesterday that they were arguing over who was going to be Superman and who was going to be Batman when they were playing superheroes.

"You're amazing," Clay whispered, taking her hand into his. "You did all of that on your own?"

"Yeah," she said. "Sometimes it was a breeze and I thought I had it all together. You know, like I could take on the whole world and do just about anything. But most days I felt like a complete failure and wondered if I was screwing everything up." Rose shrugged. "I'm guessing that I did an okay job. They both turned out pretty fantastic. Both are married now and I'm a grandmother." Rose winced at admitting that last part.

"You made a face," Clay said.

"Well, when I say things like that, it reminds me that there is quite an age difference between us. I know that I'm not supposed to say that and it's one of our rules but it's just a fact." Rose sipped the wine that Clay had poured for her. "I'm fifty years old, Clay. You making a rule to forget about our age difference won't change the fact that you're only forty."

Clay chuckled, "Only forty sounds like an oxymoron to me. It's all relative, Honey. When I look at you, I don't see a fifty-year-old grandmother. I see a sexy as fuck woman who I can't wait to get all to myself tonight." Rose felt her cheeks heat and she shyly nodded at Clay.

"Thank you for that, Clay," she said. "I guess I'll just need to work on all of that," she admitted. The waiter brought their appetizers and Clay asked if he could order dinner for her. She gladly accepted his offer and by the time dinner was over, she realized that they had spent nearly three hours talking about everything from her job to his life on the ranch and their kids. Every moment she spent with Clay only made her realize that she liked him. Hell, she was practically falling for the guy but she wouldn't ever admit that. What kind of woman lost her heart to a man she picked up in a bar and only knew for two nights? Clay was supposed to be a one time, one-night thing but he was surprisingly turning out to be so much more to her.

"How about we head back to my place," he whispered into her ear. Rose felt a shiver run down her spine at the promise she heard in his sultry voice.

"Yes," she whispered. "I'd like that."

It didn't take long to drive from the restaurant to Clay's ranch and when he pulled into his garage, she suddenly felt shy again. This world was so new to her, Rose worried that she was going to do or say something wrong and Clay would call this whole thing off between them. She so desperately wanted more of a taste of his world and she was hoping he'd give it to her.

"You know, we didn't finish our discussion about what you want to try tonight, Rose," Clay said.

"You distracted me with food, wine, and excellent conversation," Rose teased.

"How about you let me distract you with sex now?" he countered. Rose nodded and took his offered hand, following him down to the finished basement. It looked like a giant family room, complete with a bar in the corner and even a pool table. Clay tugged her along down a hallway to a room with a locked door. He pulled the key from his pocket and unlocked the door.

"Why do you keep this room locked?" she asked.

"Mainly to keep my nosey brother and my teenage daughter out. I wouldn't want Paisley stumbling across my playroom by accident. Her mother would never let me see her again if she knew I built this place." Clay turned on the lights to the room and Rose blinked, letting her eyes adjust.

"You said your wife wasn't submissive?" Rose asked.

"Ex-wife and no, she wasn't. We had other problems, too. I couldn't give her any more children and she wanted more. That was when our marriage started to turn. My telling Abi that I wanted a sub was just the last straw. She told me she couldn't live the life that I wanted and we agreed to go our separate ways. I play at a local club but built this place for more privacy."

Rose walked into the room and suddenly wanted to run and hide. "Do you bring many women down here, Clay?" she asked. Why she worried about his answer was beyond her. This thing between them wasn't a rela-tionship—it was for fun. He wanted a sub and Rose wanted to try something new. She was up for some excitement and a whole lot of fun. She deserved it.

Rose could feel Clay standing behind her. His body was so close to hers; she could feel the heat of his breath on her neck. "No," he breathed. "I just got done this room and honestly—you're the first woman I've brought down here."

Rose turned to face him, "Really?" she questioned.

"Yeah," he admitted. Clay turned the cutest shade of pink and Rose ran her hand up over his shoulders and leaned into his body.

"It's okay, Clay. You can be honest with me. I know the score—this is just for fun. I don't need pretty promises and for you to tell me that I'm the only one."

Rose meant it too but the last thing she wanted to do was listen to how many women he had brought back to his ranch to have sex with.

"Rose," he whispered. "What if I want to make you pretty promises?" Rose felt as though her heart was going to beat out of her chest. "I won't lie to you—ever. There have been other women since my divorce. I told you that I like to play at the local club and have taken on subs there. But, you're the first woman I've ever brought back to my place and the first woman to use this room with me." Rose wanted to beg him to be the last woman he'd use the room with but that would be a promise he wouldn't be able to make her. She wasn't lying when she said she didn't want him to make her pretty promises— not unless he could keep them.

"I appreciate you telling me that, Clay," she said.

"Sir," he growled. "You will call me, Sir in here, Rose,"

She smiled up at him and nodded. "Sir," she corrected. Rose looked around the room.

"Good," he whispered against her neck. "You ready to play?"

"I think so," she stuttered. "I'm not going to lie, Sir, I'm feeling a little out of my element here," she admitted.

Clay wrapped his arms around her from behind and tugged her tighter against his body. "I've got you, Honey," he said. "We can take this as slow as you need," he drawled. Her cowboy had a way of making her knees feel week and her heart flutter with just one sentence and Rose felt like a giddy schoolgirl.

"Thank you, Sir," she whispered. "I think I'd like to try that saddle," she said pointing to the corner of the room where a riding saddle was perched over the arm of a sofa. Clay chuckled in her ear. "You do like to be spanked, don't you, Rose?"

"Yes," she said. "I liked the way you spanked me last night. I wanted more."

"Oh Honey, I can give you so much more," he agreed. Clay unzipped the back of her dress and let it fall down her body. She said a little prayer of thanks that she was wearing a pair of lacy black panties and a strapless lacy bra that matched. He let his fingers trail down her body and she leaned into his touch, craving more.

"Up on the saddle, Baby," he ordered. She turned and did as he asked, gifting him with a view of her ass. It was as if all her insecurities just melted away. Clay made her feel like a goddess and Rose knew that he'd worship her body—all she had to do was let go.

Clay unhooked her bra and she gasped when he reached around her body to cup her ample breasts. "I'm going to put some nipple clamps on these," he said, tweaking her taut nipples between his fingers. Rose moaned and writhed against the saddle.

"Yes," she hissed.

"Have you ever had nipple clamps on before, Honey?" he asked.

"No," she whispered. Rose rubbed her pussy on the saddle. She was so wet and ready for him, she needed to find her release but Clay seemed to have other ideas for her.

Rose felt his loss as soon as he removed his hands

from her sensitive nipples and crossed the room to a large storage cabinet. He rummaged through the open drawer; his handsome face so stern with concentration that she almost wanted to giggle. She sat up in the saddle and watched him and when he returned to her wearing a triumphant grin and holding up something that looked more like jewelry than clamps, she couldn't help but smile back at him.

"Those are nipple clamps?" she asked.

"Yep," Clay said. He held them out for her and she ran her fingers over the pretty blue jewels that decorated the ends. "Hold your finger out," he ordered. Rose did as he asked and he clamped the little jewel onto her finger. "I can make them as tight as you like," he said. Clay tightened the clamp on her finger, making her hiss.

"I think I'll like that," she admitted.

"When I take them off," he said, pulling the clamp free from her finger. "All the blood will rush back to your nipples giving you the most wonderful pain and pleasure, all at the same time. Want to try them?"

Rose wiggled her tingling finger and smiled up at him. "Yes," she agreed. Honestly, she wanted to try everything. She looked down her body as Clay fitted the pretty little clamps to her nipples, wincing at the tingling sensation that almost felt as if it was too much. She had to admit that once she got used to the pinching weight of the clamps, she liked it. They gave just enough of a bit of pain and Rose was starting to realize that she liked the discomfort.

Clay pushed her down over the saddle, so her belly

was almost flat with the leather. "We're going to twenty," he ordered. "You will keep count, Rose."

"All right," she whispered. Clay praised her, rubbing his big hand over her ass. Her lacy panties did nothing to hide her desire from him. He dipped his fingers down and rubbed her wet pussy, moaning as he pulled them back up to her ass and gave it a firm smack. Rose loved the way he didn't hold back with her even knowing how new this all was to her.

"One," she moaned. Clay peppered her ass with terse smacks and in between each one, he'd rub her fleshy globes, while she kept count. They got to twenty rather quickly and Rose wasn't sure if she was happy or sad about Clay being done spanking her. He ran his fingers back down through her wet folds and she moaned, rubbing shamelessly on the saddle, trying to gain the friction she needed to get herself off.

"Fuck, Honey," he growled. "You're so wet and ready for me. Hold still and let me take care of you, Rose," he ordered. She tried to hold as still as humanly possible and was probably failing miserably. Clay pulled her from the saddle and onto the nearby sofa, shucking out of his jeans as quickly as humanly possible. Just before he pulled her on top of his body, he helped her out of her panties, and Rose eagerly straddled his cock.

"Please," she whimpered. Rose could tell that Clay was just as on edge as she was but he just seemed to control it a little better than she did.

"Please what, Honey," he taunted. Clay knew that she wasn't a fan of asking for what she wanted—especially not in bed.

"I need you in me," she whispered against his lips. That seemed to be all Clay needed to give her what she wanted. He lifted her onto his erection, lowering her inch by delicious inch until she was fully seated on his cock.

"So fucking good," he moaned. Rose agreed with him. She was so close to finding her release, she couldn't help but move. She rode him like she was on fire and couldn't get enough. She couldn't. Rose was sure she'd never get enough of Clay and that thought scared the crap out of her.

She cried out his name as her orgasm ripped through her and Clay pulled the nipple clamps from her sensitive breasts. It felt like a fire ripped through her and Rose shouted out once again. She loved the way Clay followed her over, pumping himself deeper inside of her and pulling her down to kiss her. His hands were everywhere as he peppered her face and lips with kisses. Rose soaked up his whispered praises and collapsed onto his chest, her quickly beating heart matching his beat.

"Perfect," he whispered and kissed her head. He was right—everything about the two of them together was perfect.

CLAYTON

They spent the whole next morning in bed and Clay had to admit, Saturday was quickly becoming his favorite day of the week. He had texted his brother and begged him to fill in for him for the day. He told Rose that he had nothing pressing that he had to get to but that was only because Ty had called in the calvary and asked some of their ranch hands to help him out for the day. Clay was for whatever worked because he didn't have any plans of getting out of bed and going out to work.

"You know, if you have to go out to the barn, I'll understand," Rose offered.

"Nope," Clay said. "I'm good right here."

"Do you usually take Saturdays off?" she asked. He wanted to tell her that he usually did but that would be a lie.

"No," he admitted. "I usually don't take a whole lot of days off. When Paisley is here, I don't work as many hours. I try to spend as much time with her as possible but she also comes out to the barn with me and hangs out while I do my chores."

"If you need, I can do the same," Rose offered.

Clay kissed the top of her head, "Thanks for that, Honey," he said.

"When will Paisley be back?" Rose asked. That was the million-dollar question because once that happened, his worlds would collide and Clay worried that he'd have to choose between spending time with Paisley and spending time with Rose. How could he do that? The circumstance hadn't happened yet but he was feeling the panic of having to make that choice.

"She's with my ex for another week," he said. "She'll be home late next weekend."

Rose snuggled into his side, "So, we have another week?" she asked. Clay wanted to tell her that they were going to have a lot longer than just a fucking week. Hell, he wanted to tell her that they didn't have an expiration date but after just two nights together, that might not be the type of declaration he should make.

"Yeah," he breathed. "Spend the week with me and let's see where this all goes," he asked. Hell, he sounded more like he was telling her what to do and maybe he was but he didn't give a fuck. He wanted time with her and if he had to demand it or even beg for it, he would.

"Are you sure?" Rose asked.

"I've never been so sure of anything in my life, Honey. I like spending time with you. I want to do more of it," he admitted.

"Me too," she agreed. "I'd love to spend the week with you, Clay. I can stop over to my townhome after work each night and grab a change of clothes." He wanted to tell her to bring over her entire closet, for all he cared, but that might be a bit too pushy for just two days in.

"Sounds good, Baby," he said. "How about I make us some breakfast and then I'll take you out to the barn and we can go for a ride?" Rose grimaced and he thought it was probably the cutest thing he'd ever seen. "I haven't been on a horse in about twenty-five years," she admitted.

"We can take it slow," he promised. "I'd love to go riding with you then, Clay."

"Perfect. I'll pack us a lunch and we can turn it into a day," he said. Clay swatted her bare ass, "Up and at em', Honey." He loved the way Rose's giggle filled his bedroom. Clay was quickly getting used to having her in his space and he wasn't sure if that was a good or bad thing.

Clay saddled up his horse and decided to let Rose ride Lulu. She was his gentlest horse and he was hoping that Rose would be able to handle her. Rose had pulled her long blond hair back in the sexy bun that she usually opted to wear to work. Every time she pulled her hair up like that, he wanted to unpin it and mess her up a little.

"Here, Honey," he offered, linking his hands together for Rose to step into for a boost.

"You don't have to help me up," Rose countered.

"It's not as easy as it looks. Besides, it gives me a chance to put my hands on that fantastic ass of yours," Clay teased. Rose gifted him with her shy smile, looking around the empty barn to make sure that no one was watching them.

"Fine," she said. Rose put her hands on his shoulders and hooked her boot in his palms, letting him give her a hand up onto Lulu. And yeah, his favorite part was running his hands all over her ass to help her up into the saddle. Flashes of the night before bombarded his overly active brain and Rose looked down at him and giggled.

"I know exactly what you're thinking," Rose almost whispered and gave him an outrageous wink.

"Yeah, it's kind of hard to forget how fucking sexy you were in my playroom last night." Clay mounted his horse Rebel and grabbed the reigns from Rose to help lead Lulu out of the barn. "You think you can remember how to hold the reigns?" he asked.

"Yep," she said. "It's like riding a bike, right?"

Clay chuckled, "That's the second time you've asked me that, Honey. No, riding a horse is a little trickier than riding a bike. Just take it slow and if you have any questions, let me know. Follow my lead."

"Yes, Sir," Rose teased. Clay started slowly and led her out to the south meadow. It had a pond and was probably his favorite place on the ranch. They had been riding for almost thirty minutes and he could tell that Rose had just about had enough. He hadn't gone easy on her ass the night before and taking her riding today might not have been the best idea.

"How about we stop here and have our picnic?" he asked. Rose nodded her agreement and he jumped down, helping Rose down from Lulu and pulling her into his arms. "You know, we have some things to talk about still," he said. Rose looked up at him like he had lost his mind.

"Like?" she asked.

"Well, your likes and dislikes about what we've done so far. And, we need to talk about what you'd like to try," he said.

"You mean sexually?" she squeaked.

Clay chuckled, "Yeah—I mean sexually. How about we get comfortable and then we can talk."

"You know, I'm starting to see a pattern with you, Clay. I've never been a prude," she said. "But, you talk about sex more than any other man I've ever met."

"I'm going to take that as a compliment, Baby," he said. "I just want to make sure that we're on the same page. The most important bond between a Dom and his submissive is trust and communication," Clay said. He had seen it one too many times, a Dom who didn't know what the hell he was doing, who ended up hurting his sub. He wouldn't do that to Rose. She deserved more from him both as her Dom and her lover.

Rose giggled, "You should," she teased. "It's quite impressive, Clay." He spread out the blanket that he brought along with him and helped her to set out the food that he had packed into a basket.

"This looks great," she said.

"It's just some sandwiches and salad," he said. "And,"

Clay reached into the basket and pulled out two wine glasses and a bottle of wine. He wasn't a wine drinker but he had a feeling that beer wasn't in Rose's wheelhouse and he wanted their little makeshift picnic to be perfect.

"Wine," Rose said. "Well, that is a nice surprise."

"I wasn't sure if you liked wine," he said. "I know you like vodka." Rose made a face and groaned. "Still not something you want to remember?"

"No," she breathed. "Honestly, I wasn't that sick the next day but let's just say that birthday drinks didn't love me as much as I loved them. I don't drink hard liquor and that night wasn't my finest. Wine is a much safer choice for me."

"Well, it's good that I stuck with my first choice then." Clay poured her a glass and handed it to her. He poured himself one and held his glass up to toast. "To us," he said.

"Us?" Rose asked. Clay worried that he had overstepped and wanted to play it cool but the look on her face had him panicking.

"Um, sure," he said. "I mean, you agreed to move in with me," Clay said.

"Temporarily," Rose corrected. "I agreed to spend the week with you to see where this thing between us is heading."

"Sure," Clay said. Her correcting him felt like a slap. "Temporarily. I won't lie, I'm hoping you'll want to stick around though." Clay smiled at her and she rolled her eyes.

"I just need to take things slowly," Rose said. "If that's not okay—"

Clay pulled her onto his lap and wrapped his free arm around her. "I never said that," he said. "We can work this any way you need, Honey. Hell, you can call all the shots here, Rose. We can go slowly and you can put whatever stipulations you need to on whatever this is between us. But, I'm hoping you'll give us a chance to become an 'us,'" Clay admitted.

"I'd like that," Rose said.

"Great," Clay said. "Now, let's talk about sex." Rose moaned and Clay playfully bit her shoulder. "You said you've Googled a few things, right?"

"Yes," she whispered.

"Is there anything you would like to try next?" he asked. The possibilities ran through his mind and he had no problem coming up with a few things he'd like to try with Rose.

She chugged her glass of wine and held it out for a refill. Clay laughed and filled it up. Rose clearly needed the liquid courage for what they were about to discuss. "Thanks," she said. "I saw this thing that looked like a wooden cross and the woman was strapped to it."

"Mmm," Clay hummed his approval. "The St. Andrew's cross. Did you like it?"

"I think so," Rose agreed. "The woman was facing her Dom, and he was flogging her." Rose almost whispered the last part and he had to admit, the thought of flogging Rose made him damn near want to swallow his tongue.

"Where did he flog her, Rose?" Clay hoarsely asked.

"Um, her breasts," Rose admitted.

"And where else?" Clay asked. Rose looked down at her empty glass and he took it from her. "Tell me," he ordered.

Clay watched her, waiting for her to give him his answer. He thought for sure that Rose wasn't going to do it when she opened her mouth and squeaked, "Her pussy."

"Fuck," Clay swore. He set their empty glasses in the basket and rolled Rose under his body. "I need you, Honey."

ROSE

"Out here?" Rose asked, looking around the empty pasture. "Won't someone see us?"

"No," Clay growled. He was working her tight t-shirt over her head, exposing the lacy white bra Rose wore. "I love this," he said, biting the fabric. She gasped and moaned when he sucked her taut nipple into his mouth through the fabric that stood in his way of having all of her.

"Up," he ordered. Rose stood and looked down at where Clay sat, panting, trying to catch his breath. "Strip," he commanded. Rose had learned that disobeying him would earn her a spanking but that wouldn't be so bad. Clay laughed. "I can see your wheels spinning, Baby," he said. "You think I'll spank your ass red if you disobey me but there are other punishments I can come up with."

"Such as?" Rose asked. She had to admit that all the possibilities made her more and more breathless.

"Well, I could work you up, get you wet and on the verge of finding your release," he said. Rose felt as if her heart was going to beat right out of her chest with every word he said. She was already wet and ready for whatever he had planned for her.

"And," she prompted.

"And, then I'll stop," Clay said. He sat back, leaning leisurely on his elbows and Rose looked him up and down.

"Stop?" she asked.

"Yep," Clay agreed. Rose moaned and unbuttoned her jeans, slowly pulling them down her long legs. "See, I knew you'd see things my way," Clay teased. He even dared to wink at her, causing Rose to giggle.

"What next, Sir?" she asked.

"Bra and panties too, Honey," Clay ordered.

Rose shyly looked around and hesitantly nodded. "All right," she stuttered.

"No one comes out here, Rose. I promise you're safe. Trust me?" Rose did, even after just a few days together, she trusted Clay.

"I do," she admitted.

"Thank you for that, Honey," he said. Clay didn't make a move to sit up and after Rose removed her bra and panties, as he ordered, and took the initiative to crawl naked onto his lap. Rose shamelessly rubbed her wet folds on his jean-clad erection as he kissed his way up her neck.

"What's this?" he questioned.

"I thought you wouldn't mind," Rose squeaked as he palmed her bare ass.

"Well, I do like what you have in mind, Honey." Before Rose could make her next move, he had her on her back and was settled between her legs. "But, I have other plans for you, Rose." Clay licked her pussy, causing her to buck and writhe from the pleasure of his mouth on her core. She needed more, but begging wasn't something she was used to doing. Rose panted out his name and when he chuckled against her pussy, his hot breath caressing her clit, she came. Rose didn't care that they were out in the middle of a field where anyone could see them. As her orgasm ripped through her, she was suddenly freed from all her inhibitions, shouting out Clay's name, begging him for everything she never knew she wanted.

"Fuck, Baby," he growled. "That was sexy as hell." Clay hovered over her, quickly pulling off his shirt and tugging his jeans down to free his erection. He lined Rose's core up with his jutting cock and thrust into her balls deep, moaning out her name.

"Clay," she whimpered. Rose was still experiencing the aftershocks of the earth-shattering orgasm he had just given her and every movement made her want to come all over again.

"You're so tight, Honey," he said. Clay pulled her limp body up to his, seating her on his thighs. Rose felt like a rag doll, completely rung out from what he had just done to her. She wrapped her arms around his shoulders and loved the way he didn't go easy on her. He was just as demanding as when he laid her out on their picnic blanket, making a meal of her body. Rose loved that he never let her hide and the way he shame-lessly took exactly what he needed from her.

Clay kissed her like he would devour her mouth, licking and sucking his way in. He roughly pumped in and out of her pussy and she couldn't hold back anymore. Rose's second orgasm felt like a wave crashing over her and she couldn't do anything but hold onto Clay and ride it out. He thrust into her body, just about lifting them both off the ground, and when he came, he whispered her name like a prayer on his sexy, full lips.

"You're mine," he growled.

"Yes," she whispered because she was, whether her mind knew it or not, her heart was his and there was nothing she could do about that, even if she wanted to.

They spent the next few days out at his ranch. Rose had gone into the office late and left early every day and she could tell that Aiden and Corbin were starting to worry about her. It was strange having their roles reversed. Usually, it was her worrying about the two of them and not the other way around. She had been the stable force in both of their lives since they were little boys and now that she was seeing Clay, that wasn't the case anymore. Rose understood the worry that she saw in both their eyes but that didn't mean she'd stop seeing her cowboy. No, she had a taste of his dominance and there would be no turning back for her. In the half a week she had spent with him, she knew that she wouldn't be able to walk away from him anytime soon. She wanted Clay—all of him and if her boys didn't understand that, well, it was just too bad.

"Mom," Corbin interrupted her daydreams about Clay, bringing her attention back to the here and now. He stood over her desk, judgmental scowl in place, Aiden by his side. Rose knew that they were both going to give her some trouble, but she didn't care. It was nearly quitting time and all she wanted to do was stop by her townhome, pick up her mail and head out to Clay's ranch.

"Boys," she countered, staring them both down. "What can I do for you?"

"We're worried about you, Rose," Aiden said. He was always the one to take lead when they were trying to present a united front. He might not be her biological son but Aiden was most like her when it came to the way he handled himself and others around him—always so practical.

"And, why's that, Aiden?" she asked. Rose stood and rounded her desk, sitting on the corner to square off with the two of them properly.

"Because you aren't acting yourself, Mom," Corbin chimed in. "Ever since your birthday, you've been acting strangely."

Rose knew what her son meant to say. "You mean, ever since I met Clay?" she retorted.

Corbin shrugged, "Well, I didn't want to make it sound like I was blaming the guy for anything. I'll save that for after you introduce us to him."

"And, that's exactly why she doesn't want to," Aiden

groaned. "You can't even give the guy a fair shake and we haven't even met him yet."

"I'll judge him fairly once I have something more concrete to go off of, man," Corbin shouted. "How do we know this guy isn't just using her, Aiden?"

Rose stood between them and felt dwarfed by their size. "She is standing right here," she challenged. "And, she doesn't like when you talk about her as if she's not in the room. I'm not being used, Corbin James. I've met a very nice man and I am enjoying his company."

"You are spending every night at his place," Corbin said.

"Are you spying on me, Son?" Rose asked.

"No," he lied. She could always tell when her boys were lying to her and now was no different. Corbin nudged Aiden, "He is," Corbin said, throwing his best friend under the bus.

"Thanks, asshole," Aiden growled. "I've stopped by your townhouse a few times and you haven't been home."

"At eleven o'clock at night, Mom," Corbin added. "He stopped by at eleven and you weren't home. You go to bed at like eight every night. What are we supposed to think?"

"First of all, you don't need to think at all about me, boys," Rose said. She felt mad enough to put them both in time out and take away all their electronics, just like when they were little. But, she was dealing with grown men who should both know better than to stick their noses in her business.

"Second—who's to say that I'm not still in bed by

eight?" she taunted. Rose almost giggled at the groans and disgusted faces they both made.

"Seriously, Rose," Aiden moaned. "We don't need the mental picture of what you're doing with your mystery man."

"Well, then don't stick your nose where it doesn't belong, Aiden," she challenged. "What I'm doing, where I am, and who I'm with is neither of your business. To quote you both, 'I'm a grown-ass woman who doesn't need you in my business,'" Rose laughed at the shocked expressions they both wore. "Isn't that what you two like to tell me?"

"Yeah," Aiden breathed. Corbin shot him a look and he shrugged. "Well, she's got us up against the ropes, man. We do tell her that all the time. Maybe it's time to let your mom fly the nest and find her way," Aiden said. Rose giggled at the way he threw her words back at her. She always told them that they needed to do that whenever they asked her for her advice. Sure, she'd willingly give them her two cents but she also wanted her boys to find their ways. It's why they had been so successful in business and how they found the perfect women and were in loving relationships with beautiful kids. They were given the chance to find their ways and she was so proud of them both.

"I love you both, so much," she whispered. "But, now it's my time to find some happiness. Clay makes me happy," she admitted.

"Are you in love with him?" Corbin asked. He sounded more like he was accusing her of something than asking her a question.

"It's much too early in our relationship for something like that, Corbin," she lied. She had already fallen in deep with Clay and if she was being completely honest with herself and her boys, she had fallen in love with him. But, admitting that out loud would only make her sound like a lunatic.

"I think we're just curious about the guy you're spending your time with, Rose," Aiden offered.

"Younger guy," Corbin chimed in.

Rose sighed in frustration. "His age has nothing to do with any of this," Rose countered. "This is going nowhere and if you both don't mind; I'd like to close down my computer for today and call it. I have some errands to run before—" She almost said before she went home to Clay's ranch but then she'd have to admit that she had temporarily moved in with him and that wasn't something she planned on telling them. At least, not until things became more permanent in her living situation.

"Before you go spend the night at your boyfriends?" Corbin taunted. She refused to go another round with her son. Rose knew that was exactly what he wanted.

"Look," Aiden cut in. "How about you just let us meet the guy and then we'll back off some."

"Some?" Rose asked. "How about you back off completely?"

"That's not going to happen, Mom. I've told you this before and I meant it. You're my business. You're both of our business and we'll check in on you whether you like it or not," Corbin said.

"He's right, Rose," Aiden agreed. "Even though he

could use some work on his delivery, I agree with Corbin. We love you and will always keep an eye on you. That's all we're getting at. Just let us meet the guy to see for ourselves that he's not some crazed killer that wants to drag you off to the woods to murder you," Aiden teased. Rose smiled but Corbin seemed less amused by Aiden's theatrics. He groaned, running his hands through his blond hair, making it stand on end. Rose went up on her tiptoes and smoothed his hair back into place.

"If I agree to let you meet him, will you two agree to give me some space. I like this man and I'd like to see where this thing between us is going. I can't do that with you two hovering over me like two mother hens." Rose framed her son's face with her hands, forcing him to look her in her eyes. "Please," she asked.

Corbin closed his blue eyes, shutting her out and when he opened them again, she could see his resolve. Her son wasn't going to easily back down but he'd let her win this battle.

"Fine," he conceded. "If we get to meet him and he checks out, I promise to give you some space, Mom," he agreed.

Rose turned to face Aiden and he smiled and nodded his agreement before she even asked her question. "Me too," he said. "But, I will probably still check in on you from time to time," he amended.

"Fair enough," she said, kissing Aiden's cheek. "I love you boys but I need to get going." Rose scurried around her work area, turning things off and shutting down for the day. "How does Saturday sound—you know, to meet Clay?"

"I'll check with Zara, but I think I can make it. You just want me and Corbin or the whole crew?" God, the thought of Corbin and Aiden bringing their wives and all their kids to meet Clay was a scary one.

"How about just you and Corbin this time and then we can get everyone involved once I have a clearer understanding of what's happening between the two of us?" Rose asked. Corbin and Aiden both agreed. "Good, and you'll have a chance to meet Clay's daughter, Paisley. She'll be home from her mother's that night and I'll be meeting her for the first time." Clay had sprung that little surprise on her that morning, just before she left for work and she had been a nervous wreck all day.

"How old is his daughter?" Corbin asked.

"Thirteen," Rose squeaked. "And, from what I understand, she's a handful. I don't know that I agree with Clay on this but he's not telling Paisley about me until we meet, face to face. I think he's afraid his daughter won't come home if she knows what she's walking into." Aiden's long whistle rang through the small office.

"This is going to be a shit show," he said.

Corbin laughed and shook his head. "I think you just bit off more than you'll be able to chew, Mom," he teased. "I'll be there Saturday. I wouldn't miss this show for anything." Rose grabbed her things and headed for the elevator.

"I'll be out tomorrow," she said. "Your calendar isn't too busy, Aiden and you and Zara are taking my grandson to the park for the day," she told Corbin. "I'll text you both Clay's address. Let's say you boys get there by six and I'll have a little something for dinner," Rose said. She knew that food always made Corbin and Aiden more agreeable.

"See you Saturday," Aiden called as the elevator doors closed. Rose wasn't sure what she had just agreed to but one thing was perfectly clear—Aiden was right. Saturday was going to be a complete shit show.

CLAYTON

Clay worried that they were rushing things introducing their kids into the equation. He and Rose had only known each other for a week now but he already knew how he felt about her. He was in love with her but telling her that wasn't going to fly. No, his Rose was too practical to hear him say the words out loud. He hoped that she could feel the way he felt about her every time he touched her and see it in his eyes every time he looked at her. God, he wished that they were at the point that he could make some sweeping declaration and not have his woman freak out but that would just take time. He could be patient if that's what it took because Rose was worth it. Clay wanted to spend the rest of his life with her and he'd wait forever, if that's what it would take.

"Corbin and Aiden will be here any minute," Rose said. She was scurrying around his kitchen and he loved the way she looked in his home. She hadn't gone back to her place since their second night together. She had stopped by her townhome to pick up essentials like clothing and personal items. Other than those few trips home, she was staying at his place twenty-four, seven and he loved that she was so comfortable with him and his ranch. If tonight went as planned, Clay wanted to ask her to make it official and just move in with him.

"Well, this is quite a spread you put on for the kids, Honey," Clay teased.

"I am fierce when it comes to ordering out," she said. Rose giggled and he couldn't help his smile. Her good mood was infectious.

"What's so funny?" he asked.

"You calling my boys, 'kids,'" she said. "They're almost as old as you are." They had already been over everyone's ages a few times and he hated how she kept reminding him of their age difference. It didn't matter to him—none of that crap did.

"You know it doesn't bother me, right?" Clay questioned. He caged Rose against the counter, effectively trapping her. "You keep breaking our new rule number one," he whispered into her ear.

"I know," she said. Rose leaned back against his body and sighed. "It's just hard not to think about our age difference. I'm just hoping that my boys can see past it. I'm worried that this is a bad idea," she admitted.

"If we're being completely honest here, Baby, I'm worried too. I've never introduced Paisley to any of my women friends," he said. There wasn't any other woman that he felt this way about besides his ex, but he'd keep that bit of information to himself. "I'm worried she won't be very receptive to meeting the new woman in my life."

"Have you had many women friends that you would have wanted to introduce your daughter to?" Rose asked. He could hear the uncertainty in her question and he hated that he made her feel that way.

"No," he honestly admitted. "You know that I played at the local club, even took on a few subs but there was never a woman I cared enough about to introduce to Paisley—that is until now. You're so much more than a friend, Honey."

"You care about me?" she asked. It pissed Clay off that Rose didn't already know that.

"I more than care about you, Rose," he said. "I think I'm falling for you." He was a coward. Clay was taking the chicken's way out and he owed her so much more than that. He had made her a promise to give him only her honesty and here he was hiding behind half-truths, lurking in the shadows of his fear.

The knock at the door startled them both back to reality and she turned to face him, finally looking him in the eyes. "That must be the boys," she whispered. He wanted to tell her to let them wait. Clay wanted to convince her that they were good for each other and that he was more than falling for her—he was already in love with her. He wanted to ask her if she felt the same way about him and demand that she share her feelings with him, but he knew that pushing Rose wouldn't end well for either of them.

Rose crossed the family room and opened the front door to let Aiden and Corbin into his house. Clay watched as they hugged Rose and protectively flanked her sides as they walked back to the kitchen. "Boys," she said. "This is Clay." He rounded the center island and held out his hand.

"Aiden Bentley." He shook Clay's extended hand and smiled. "Good to meet you," Aiden said.

"You too," Clay said. He turned to Corbin and held out his hand noting the indifferent scowl Rose's son wore compared to Aiden. Clay stood there for what felt like forever before Rose cleared her throat. It was a clear warning and her son backed down. He reluctantly shook Clay's hand and grumbled his name.

"Corbin Eklund." Clay noticed that his handshake was more like a tug of war than a handshake. The guy was as big as a mountain and if he wasn't Rose's son, he'd be weary of crossing paths with him.

"It's nice to meet you, Corbin," Clay said. "Your mom has told me so much about you—both of you."

"Well, I hope she hasn't told you everything about us. I mean, we've done some pretty questionable things over the years," Aiden joked. Clay had to admit, he liked the guy. He was at least trying to lighten the mood whereas Corbin seemed to want to rip Clay apart and ask questions after.

Rose giggled, "You boys were the worst growing up. You still cause me trouble but I wouldn't change a thing because you both turned out to be pretty fantastic."

"You're not wrong. I am pretty fantastic," Aiden teased. Corbin still hadn't said more than his name to Clay and he was wondering if the big guy would ever chime in. They followed Rose to the kitchen and she pulled out two beers and handed them across the counter to the guys and one to Clay.

"Thanks, Honey," he said, taking the bottle from her.

"I have questions," Corbin grumbled.

"Shit, man," Aiden complained. "You couldn't wait until we have dinner or something? You agreed not to fuck this up for Rose."

"Language," Rose chided. "Clay's daughter will be here in about thirty minutes and I can't have you talking like that, Aiden."

"Sorry," Aiden grumbled.

"And you," Rose said, pointing her finger into Corbin's massive chest. "Whatever you want to ask, do it now because once Paisley gets here, I won't have you causing trouble."

Corbin nodded and turned to Clay, staring him down. "Why are you with my mother?" Corbin asked, jumping right to the heart of it all.

Clay took a swig of his beer and wrapped his arm around Rose's waist. "Because your mom is a fantastic person. I care for your mom, very much," he admitted.

Corbin barked out his laugh and set his bottle down on the counter with a thud. "In just a week?" he asked. "You care about my mother, very much, in just one week?"

Clay shrugged, "I know that sounds crazy but yes," Clay said. "The night we met; I was wallowing in self-pity. I was turning forty and feeling bad for myself. When I met your mom, she was going through the same thing and—"

"No," Corbin all but shouted. "She wasn't going

through the same thing. My mother turned fifty, not forty. You do realize that, right?" Clay wanted to deck the guy for being such an ass. He hated the shame and embarrassment that he saw in Rose's eyes.

"Corbin," Aiden said. "That's not fair."

"If you're asking if I know that Rose is ten years older than I am—sure. She was upfront with me about everything. But, our age difference isn't something that we've chosen to focus on. Just because you choose not to understand our relationship doesn't mean that it won't work for us. I personally don't give a fuck about how old your mom is. If you have a problem with it then that's on you." He tugged Rose closer and kissed her forehead.

"What are your intentions with my mom?" Corbin asked. Man, the guy wasn't going to quit. He didn't seem happy with any of Clay's answers. He hated how badly this evening was going but he wouldn't let Rose's son ruin their plans. He still had to get through introducing his daughter to Rose and he worried that Paisley was going to have the same reaction to the new woman in his life as Corbin had about him.

"That's enough, Corbin," Rose chided. "I asked you both to come here tonight to meet Clay, not to have you tear him down for wanting to be a part of my life."

"I'm just saying that this has all happened a little fast, Mom," Corbin countered.

"Well, as you so politely pointed out, Son, I'm fifty years old. I don't have much time left to waste." Aiden tried to muffle his laugh and failed. Corbin shot him a look like he wanted to tear him apart and Aiden had the good sense to back down, even holding his hands up as if in surrender.

"She's got you there, man," Aiden said.

"Your mom and I haven't figured out what our intentions are. We're feeling this out as we go," Clay admitted. "All I know is I like spending time with your mom, Corbin. I hope you can come to understand that I have no bad intentions or plan on hurting your mother in any way."

Rose shrugged, "We're just having fun," she added. Clay wanted to protest and tell them that she wasn't just someone he was having fun with. Rose was quickly becoming so much more to him but that was something he might want to share with her first.

Paisley came running in through the front door and Rose shot Corbin a look. "Behave yourself. Clay's daughter is just a kid," she reminded. "Act like the grown men you are."

Aiden crossed his heart and smiled, "Promise," he agreed.

"You're such a suck up," Corbin groaned. Clay released Rose and met Paisley in the family room to pull her in for a big hug. It had been a week and a half since he saw his daughter and he had to admit—he missed the hell out of her.

"I missed you, Squirt," he said, squeezing her extra tight.

"Dad," Paisley moaned. "I can't breathe." Clay chuckled and released his daughter.

"Sorry, Squirt. How was your Mom's?" he asked.

"Good," Paisley said.

She never really elaborated on what she did at her mom's house. It was almost as if she was afraid to talk about her mother in front of him no matter how many times he insisted that he didn't mind. He wanted to hear about all parts of his daughter's life, not just the time she spent under his roof.

"Did Daisy have her baby yet?" she asked. Daisy was Paisley's favorite horse on the farm and she had been ready to drop her foal for days now.

"Nope," he said. "But, it should be any day now."

"I'm glad I didn't miss it," Paisley said.

"Come on in the kitchen," Clay said. "I've got some people I want you to meet." He had run Paisley meeting Rose past Abi. It was something they always agreed to do but this was the first time he had an occasion to talk to his ex about their daughter meeting a new woman in his life. His ex seemed fine with it all but told him to call her if Paisley needed to talk. He knew their daughter was closer with her mom. She was a thirteen year old girl and that just seemed par for the course. Still, it stung a little that Paisley would need to turn to her mom when she got upset. He wanted to be there for his daughter too but he somehow felt ill equipped to do so.

"Paisley, this is Corbin and Aiden." His daughter shook both of their offered hands and smiled.

"Nice to meet you, Paisley," Aiden said.

"What's up, kid?" Corbin casually asked.

"Not much," she answered. "Do you two work with my dad?" Corbin shot Clay a look and shook his head.

"Nope," he said. Clay could tell from Corbin's smart assed smirk that he was going to enjoy this next part.

"Your dad and my mom are dating," he said. Clay wanted to curse inwardly but kept his cool. Now was not the time to start a fight with Corbin. He needed to keep his head and they would all get through this fucked up evening.

"Dating?" Paisley looked at him as if he had lost his mind. "What's he talking about, Dad?" she asked.

"Well," Clay said, clearing his throat. "I was getting to that part." He glared at Corbin and the big guy had the nerve to smile back at him, crossing his arms over his massive chest. Yeah, Corbin didn't give a fuck that he had just messed up their plans.

"I'm Rose." She held out her hand for Paisley to shake and his daughter just stood there, looking at her offered hand as if she didn't understand what to do next.

"Paisley, this is the woman I'm seeing. This is Rose," Clay said. Paisley took a step back from Rose's hand and when she realized that his daughter wasn't going to shake her hand, she dropped it back to her side.

"What about mom?" Paisley asked.

"You know that your mom and I aren't together anymore, Paisley," Clay said. "We haven't been for a long time."

"So, you're just going to replace her?" Paisley challenged.

"Maybe we should give you both some privacy," Rose asked. "That way you can talk through all of this."

"No," Clay said. "Paisley, you know that your mother and I are no longer together. Rose is going to be around here a lot and you'll need to get used to that fact. She's a part of my life now."

"Well, if she's going to be staying here, then I won't be," Paisley picked up her backpack and stomped off to her bedroom. Clay wanted to go after her and tell her to go back into the kitchen and apologize but he also knew his daughter well enough to know that would do him no good. Paisley was a lot like him and when she lost her temper, it was best to let her work through some of her anger and give her time to cool off.

"Should you go after her?" Rose asked.

"No," he said. "I'm so sorry," he whispered.

"Well, this has been fun. I can't say that I'm surprised at how things have turned out," Corbin said. "Honestly, mom, you've known him for a week and you expected us to all just be okay with this?" Corbin waved his arms around like a crazy person as if trying to drive his point home.

"That's not fair, Corbin," Aiden challenged. "Rose has given up so much for us, maybe you should try to meet her halfway."

Rose held up her hand, effectively stopping Aiden from saying more. "While I appreciate you trying to help, Aiden, it's not necessary. Sink or swim, I'll take care of myself and clean up my own messes. I'll be taking a week's vacation, effective immediately. I need some time to think about a few things." Clay worried that he was one of the things Rose needed to think about. "If you need me, I'll be right here." She linked her fingers with his, giving him some comfort.

Paisley stomped back out to the kitchen from her

room, another bag slung over her shoulder. "Mom is coming to pick me back up. I won't stay here as long as that woman is in our house," she said, pointing her little finger at Rose for good measure. "I'll stay at Mom's—she said it's all right with her."

"That isn't for you to decide, Paisley. Your mother and I discuss this stuff together," Clay shouted. He knew he was letting his anger at the way their night had blown up, get the better of him. He didn't mean to take it out on his daughter but she was acting like a complete brat.

"If you need me to go," Rose whispered.

"No," he said, not letting her even finish her thought. "My daughter needs to learn some manners, as does your son. They should be the ones to leave. As for you, Paisley, I'll be calling your mom and we'll be discussing a punishment for the way you've acted tonight. You might not like the fact that I'm dating but you don't get to be rude to guests in our home. I'm disappointed. We raised you to be better than this." Paisley stared him down, challenge bright in her hazel eyes.

A car honked out in the driveway and Paisley turned to leave. "That's mom," she said over her shoulder. She was leaving without even saying goodbye to him. "Let me know when she's gone and I'll come home. Take care of Daisy for me." Paisley walked out the front door and before he heard Abi's truck even leave the driveway, his phone chimed. He pulled it from his pocket and saw that his ex had tried to call him three times.

"I need to call Abi and work this out," he said to

Rose. "It was nice to meet you both," he lied, nodding to Aiden and Corbin.

"You too, Clay," Aiden said. "Good luck with everything." Corbin didn't say a word, just stared him down as he left the room. The last thing Clay heard was Corbin's muddled curses after Rose slapped him and he couldn't help but smile to himself. It had been a complete cluster fuck of a night but the one thing that got him through was having Rose by his side. They might all be right—it might be too soon for him to feel the way he did about Rose but Clay didn't give a fuck. She was his and there was no way he was going to let either of their kids come between them.

ROSE

"What the hell is wrong with you?" Rose whispered to her son. "I can't believe I'm saying this but you acted worse than a thirteen-year-old girl tonight, Corbin." Aiden laughed and Rose slapped his arm. "And you," she said. "You should have warned me that Corbin was acting like an ass before you got here. A head's up would have been nice, Aiden. How many times a day do I save your ass?"

"Geeze," Aiden grumbled. "A thousand times a day. You're right," he offered. "I'm sorry but I had no idea he was going to be this bad."

"What's going on with you that you acted out like this, Corbin?" Rose asked.

"I'm not a child, Mom and I wasn't 'acting out,' as you like to call it. I guess when I saw how young your new boy toy is, I lost my shit. You do realize he's closer to my age than he is yours, right?" Corbin taunted. She was well aware of that fact but she was also trying to forget their age difference, as Clay ordered.

"He's not my 'boy toy,' Corbin," she chided. "Age has nothing to do with what's happening here. You acted like an overbearing ass," Rose said.

"You know when she cusses that you're in deep shit," Aiden teased.

"I know," Corbin said. "I just don't want you to get hurt, Ma," he said. Rose wrapped her arms around her son's waist.

"I'm finally having some fun, living the life I want to live. If you can't be happy for me, Corbin, then just be civil. That's all I ask," Rose said.

"So, get on the Clay bandwagon or stay the fuck out of your way?" Corbin asked. "Basically," Rose agreed. "It's finally my time to be happy. Raising you boys brought me so much joy and you've turned out to be such good men. I love you both, so much. I love the women you've chosen to build your lives and families with. I just want a chance to find that same happiness."

"You're right, Rose," Aiden said. "You do deserve your shot at happiness. I'm team Clay all the way," he agreed.

Rose hugged him, "Thanks, Aiden," she said. They both turned to look at Corbin and he dramatically threw his arms in the air.

"Fine," he grumbled. "I'll give him a chance. I won't pretend to be happy about any of this or to like him, but I'll try."

"Thank you, Son," Rose said. "That's all I ask."

"We need to get going," Aiden said, checking his watch. "Sorry about dinner," he said.

Rose looked at the untouched food and sighed. "It's

fine," she said. "I'll wrap it up for later. You guys go home to your families." Rose walked them out.

"You still taking the week off?" Aiden asked.

"Yes," she said. "I just need some time to think things over. Is that okay?"

"Sure," Aiden said. "I'll get a temp for the week and we'll muddle through." Rose giggled when he made a face and kissed them both goodnight. She watched as their headlights disappeared down the long drive and turned to walk back into the house. She could hear Clay still on his call and wanted to give him some privacy, so she started to put away all the food she had ordered.

"Fine," she heard him bark. "I'll let you know." Clay ended his call and tossed his cell onto the counter.

"Everything all right?" Rose asked. "No," Clay said. "Paisley is really upset and now Abilene wants to meet you. Apparently, my daughter fed my ex some bullshit that you were mean to her. I told her you didn't have a mean bone in your body, but—"

Rose giggled and covered her hand over her chest, "Your ex-wife didn't believe you?"

"No," Clay breathed. "She said our daughter wouldn't be this upset over nothing."

"Well, this is hardly nothing. You introduced your thirteen-year-old daughter to the first woman you've been dating. I'm sure it was a complete shock to her."

"I don't know that I'd call what we've been doing, 'dating,' Rose," Clay said. She thought it was cute the way he used air quotes around the word, "Dating". She wouldn't necessarily call what they had been doing dating either but she wasn't sure what the correct term was.

"What would you call it, then?" she asked.

"Um," Clay stalled. He even tapped his finger to his chin and Rose smiled. She wrapped her arms around his waist and he pulled her tighter against his body. "Well, there's been a heck of a lot of sex," he teased.

"Yes," she agreed. "There has been quite a bit of that. And, we did go out to your favorite steak house for our second night together," she offered.

"Yep," he said. "I think it's time to take this thing to the next level," he whispered.

"Next level?" Rose questioned. "We've known each other for seven days now. Don't you think we're jumping ahead of ourselves?"

"Well, we did just introduce our kids to each other," Clay reminded. "I'd say that you moving in with me is just the next natural step."

"Moving in with you?" Rose repeated.

"You know, you're repeating what I say an awful lot," Clay said. "I stand by what I told your son, Rose. I don't give a fuck how long we've known each other or what our age difference is. What's happening between us just feels right and I don't want to wait to be with you just because that's what other people think we should do. I want to move forward with what's next. Move in with me—permanently?" he asked. Rose took a step back from him, not missing the disappointment in his eyes as she did.

"I—I just don't know if that's a good idea," she said. "What happens if you change your mind in a month?"

"Won't happen," Clay assured her. She looked at him like he lost his mind. If she gave up her townhome to move in with him and this thing between them didn't work out, she'd be homeless. Rose was too old to be so reckless. No—old wasn't the correct word. Mature—she was too mature to just jump in feet first and not think about the consequences.

"Okay—let's compromise," Clay offered.

"That sounds fair," Rose agreed. "I love a good meeting of the minds. What are you thinking?"

"Well, how about you move enough stuff here, to stay with me on my ranch and not have to run back to your townhouse every few days? That way we can take what's happening between us for a test drive—what do you think?" Clay watched her and God, he looked so hopeful, she couldn't tell him no. Plus, she kind of liked the idea of a test run. She could save some time every day not having to run by her place and she'd have more time to spend with Clay when his day was done on the ranch.

"I'd say we could live at your townhome but then I'd have to find someone to take over my early morning and evening chores around here. Ty already does more than his share around here. But, if that's what it takes to get you to agree to live with me, I'll gladly move my shit over to your townhome." Rose smiled up at him and shook her head.

"Nope," she said. "I know how much you love your ranch and it would be silly for us to cram into my tiny townhome. Your place is so much bigger," she said. "I'll move some of my stuff over this weekend," she offered.

Clay picked her up and spun her around his kitchen, making her squeal. "You've made me so happy, Baby," he said. "Thank you."

"Let's see how you feel after spending the next week with me. I have a week off from work, don't forget," Rose said.

"So, you aren't going in to work this week?" Clay asked.

"No," Rose breathed. "I think it's for the best. Corbin needs to calm down and honestly, I could use a little breathing room myself."

"Well then, I have another proposition for you," Clay offered.

"Wow," Rose teased, "I'm not sure I can handle more, Clay."

He chuckled and kissed the side of her neck, right on her ticklish spot. She giggled and swatted at him. "Go with me to Texas," he said.

"Texas?" she asked.

"Yeah, I have two auctions for my cattle in Austin this week and I'd love to show you my home away from home." Rose knew that getting out of town might not be such a bad idea. She'd let things calm down and then they could come back fresh and deal with their kids and whatever this was that was happening between them.

"When do we leave?" Rose asked.

"You mean, you'll go with me?" Clay asked. Rose smiled and nodded.

"I just need to pack up my stuff and move it over here and then I should run by the office and let the boys know I'm going out of town for a few days."

"You sure that's a good idea?" he asked.

"Yeah, it's the right thing to do. I need to at least tell Aiden where I'll be. Just in case I'm needed while we're gone." Rose finished putting away the rest of the dinner that no one touched and turned to face him. "That just leaves us with what to do about me meeting your ex-wife."

Clay looked like he wanted to say something but closed his mouth. "You sure you're up for that too?" he asked. Rose crossed the kitchen and wrapped her arms around Clay.

"I'm up for just about anything with you by my side," she said.

"Well, that's good because Abi just messaged me that she dropped Paisley off at her mom's house and was stopping by here in a few minutes. Now's your chance to run," he teased although Rose was pretty sure he wasn't joking.

"I'm good," she lied. "How about I give you guys a few minutes to talk things over and then I'll join you after my shower?" Rose knew that meeting his ex-wife at the front door, presenting a united front might make Abi feel as though they are ganging up on her and that was the last thing Rose wanted.

"I think that might be a good idea," Clay admitted. "Just don't take too long—I'd like to get this over with and celebrate the fact that you've agreed to move in with me."

"Deal," Rose agreed.

❄

She had spent a good thirty minutes in the shower, hiding from having to meet Clay's ex-wife. Having to face the woman he spent so much of his life with; the woman who gave him a child, made Rose want to run and hide. But, she agreed to meet with Abi and talk through what happened tonight. She just hoped that she had wasted enough time showering and drying her hair to give Clay time to smooth things over. Rose pulled on her robe and walked back out to the kitchen. As soon as she heard Abi shouting at Clay, she wanted to turn back around and go back to the bedroom to hide.

"You let her walk right into an ambush," Abi yelled.

"I know and maybe that wasn't the best way to handle all of this. I was worried that if I told Paisley about Rose, she wouldn't come home. Plus, Roses boys were here and I thought it would help soften the blow, meeting them too."

"Boys—she has kids? How old are they?" Abi asked.

"Thirty-three," Rose said, turning the corner to walk into the kitchen. "I have a son who's thirty-three and I also raised his best friend, whom I consider a son. He's the same age." Rose held her hand out to Abi who seemed too shocked to do anything but openly stare at her with her mouth gaped open. "I'm Rose Eklund."

When Rose realized that Abi wasn't going to shake her hand, she dropped it back to her side. Clay cleared his throat and pulled Rose against his side, wrapping his arm protectively around her.

"This is my ex-wife, Abilene," he said.

Abi seemed to find her tongue and stuck her hand out in Rose's direction. "Abi Nash," she said, putting special emphasis on her last name. Rose knew that the other woman was marking her territory. Clay had already admitted to her that he had never brought another woman around Abi or Paisley—she was the first. This all had to be so new and disturbing for his ex, Rose almost felt sorry for the woman. She shook Abi's hand and plastered her best fake smile on her face.

"It's good to meet you, Abi," Rose said. "I'm sorry about what happened here tonight. Clay and I were just trying to introduce our kids to each other and it seems to have backfired. My son wasn't very receptive to meeting Clay either."

Abi sneered at her and Rose knew she wasn't going to like what she said even before she said it. "I can understand where your son is coming from. I mean, he and Clay are practically the same age. Isn't Ty about thirty-three?" Yeah—her question was laced with what felt like a slap in the face.

Clay flexed his fingers in Rose's side and smiled down at her. "Tyler is thirty-two," he said, shrugging as if it wasn't any big deal. "They might have all gone to school together," he said. Rose hadn't thought about that, but it was probably true.

"You weren't far in front of them," Abi continued. "In school that is."

"Don't Abi," Clay all but shouted. "I know what you're hinting at and Rose being older than me has nothing to do with any of this. What the three of us are here to discuss is what happened with Paisley tonight. Our daughter was rude to both Rose and me and she has to know she can't treat adults that way."

"Our daughter is a matter for you and me to discuss, Clay. Rose has no business in what we decide to do about Paisley's rudeness." Abi countered. Rose pulled free from Clay's side and nodded.

"It was good to meet you, Abi. I hope to see you again," Rose said, turning to go back to Clay's bedroom. She wouldn't insert herself into their private conversation no matter how bad it felt to be dismissed by his ex.

"Rose, wait," he ordered. She stopped short and Abi gasped.

"It all makes sense now," Abi whispered. "She's what you wanted me to become. Oh—what did you call it again? Submissive, right?" Clay shot Abi a look and Rose stared him down.

"Yes, Clay?" Rose questioned.

"Dear God, I'm right aren't I?" Abi went on. "Women aren't meant to be pathetic, meek little mice, obeying their masters. You've set our cause back by at least a hundred years, Rose."

"Don't talk to her that way. You have no right to stand in my home and question me about my relationship with Rose. It has nothing to do with you," Clay spat.

"This used to be my home too and it's still our daughter's if she chooses to ever come back here," Abi said, standing her ground. Abi was so different from what she expected. Rose thought that Clay was exaggerating when he said that his ex didn't have a submissive bone in her body, but he wasn't. Knowing how dominant Clay was with her made Rose's heart ached for him, knowing that he had to hide who he was for so long.

"You have no right to treat Rose like she's done something wrong because of who she is. She gives me what I never got from you. Rose has made me realize what I've been missing all these years," Clay said.

"Clay," Rose whispered. "It's all right. You're right, Abi. I am submissive and I do take orders from Clay. But, it's not because I'm a meek mouse, as you put it. I don't bow to his dominance or take power away from myself or any other woman, for that matter. Being Clay's submissive gives me all the power in our relationship. He might call the shots but I get to decide what I want to give and not give in our relationship. You wouldn't understand that, though because you aren't submissive. That's okay too. We're all different and Clay just found someone he can be himself with."

"What the hell does that mean? Are you saying that my husband couldn't be himself with me?" Abi asked.

"Clay's your ex-husband, Abi. And, yes. He had to hide a part of who he was with you and that makes me sad for you both. You both deserve to find people who make you happy and give you what you need." Rose boldly walked back across the kitchen to kiss Clay. She could feel Abi's eyes boring into her like laser beams and she almost wanted to laugh.

"I'll be waiting for you in our bedroom," Rose said. She knew she wasn't playing fairly, but she didn't care anymore.

"So, she's living here now?" Abi started back in as soon as Rose turned the corner to go down the hallway.

She smiled to herself when she heard Clay's simple answer.

"Yep," he said. "And if I have my way, it will be a permanent situation."

Rose heard Abi's gasp as she shut herself away in the master suite. She trusted Clay to handle his ex and now that they all knew exactly where each other stood, she had no doubt he'd be coming to find her in his bed, sooner than later. She'd give him a little surprise and be waiting for him naked. It was what he told her he'd like from her every night that she slept in his bed—her completely naked and ready for him. It was the least Rose could do for Clay, after all—he was her Dom.

CLAYTON

Clay booked an extra plane ticket for Rose to go with him on his business trip to Austin and then turned off the lights in his office and trudged back to bed. It had been a long ass day and he was ready to wrap his arms around Rose and sleep for days.

He and Abi had worked out that Paisley would be grounded from her electronics for a week for her rude behavior. He was happy that his ex at least saw the way their daughter treated Rose and him as unacceptable behavior and agreed to discipline her. Unfortunately, her compliance came at a cost to him—Paisley would be staying at her mom's house until they could work this whole mess out. He agreed that forcing her to be at the ranch with Rose when she didn't want to be, wasn't the answer.

Abi left shortly after Rose went back to their bedroom. His ex realized that there was nothing left to say to him to convince Clay that he was making a mistake. Rose wasn't a mistake. She was the best fucking thing to ever happen to him, besides his daughter. They both came up with a punishment for Paisley, agreed to all the terms of her staying with Abi and he showed his ex-wife out. The only thing left to do was to buy Rose's plane ticket before she could change her mind about going with him to Texas on business. She had already told her boys that she was taking next week off, so there wasn't anything to stand in her way but self-doubt and fear that Abi was right. Clay wouldn't allow that to happen and booking her ticket was the only sure-fire way to make sure Rose followed through with their plans.

He crept into their room, the lights were all out and he could hear Rose's gentle breathing from her side of the bed. She had fallen asleep waiting for him. Clay quickly brushed his teeth and decided to take a shower before crawling into bed. He had just stepped into the hot spray of the shower when Rose sleepily walked into his master bathroom, blinking against the light. She wore nothing but a smile and when he opened the shower door, in invitation for her to join him, she immediately took him up on his offer.

"Hey," she whispered, as he pulled her against his wet body.

"Hey yourself," he said back. "You okay, Baby?" Clay worried that Abi's criticisms were a bit harsh for Rose.

"Yeah," she breathed. "Sorry I fell asleep. I was trying to wait up for you."

"It's fine," he said. "Abi left a bit ago and I had to buy your plane ticket for Austin." Rose smiled up at him and snuggled against his body.

"When do we leave?" she asked.

"How does tomorrow sound?" he asked. "I'd like to get out of here and put today as far behind us as possible."

"That sounds like heaven," Rose agreed. "I'll just need to tell the boys that I'm heading out of town. And well, I need to check in on Corbin."

Clay wanted to tell her that her son could use a time-out like Paisley but things were a little different with Corbin being a grown man.

"All right," he agreed. "You want me to go with you?"

"No," she said. "I think it would be best if I sat down with my son and we had a little heart to heart. He can't treat you like he did tonight—I won't allow it."

"Thanks for that, Honey," Clay said. "Abi and I agreed that Paisley should stay with her for a bit. You know, until she gets used to us being an us. She's grounded though."

"I'm sorry, Clay," Rose said. "I hate that it's come to this." "She'll come around," he offered. "My daughter's stubborn, but she's also fair."

"Gee, I wonder if she gets that from you or your ex," Rose teased. She had a point, both of them were pretty damn stubborn.

"Funny," he said, swatting her ass.

"Well, the apple didn't fall far from either tree," Rose teased. "I wish I could just ground Corbin for acting like an ass but I'm not sure that will work. He'll come around too. If he doesn't, I'll get his wife, Ava involved and she'll set him straight." Clay chuckled, "It's hard to believe that anyone could set your son straight. He's a big guy."

"He is," Rose agreed. "But, he's a big teddy bear."

"Well, the bear part is probably right," Clay teased.

"How about I get up early tomorrow and go over to Corbin's and deal with my ferocious bear?" Rose said. "Then, I'll meet you back here and we can head to Austin."

"Now, that sounds like a deal to me," Clay agreed. He pushed Rose through the hot spray of the shower and up against the cold tile of the shower wall. "How about we negotiate another deal, my beautiful sub?" he asked. Clay kissed down her neck and back up to her mouth giving her hot, wet kisses. Rose daringly wrapped her hands around his erection, eliciting a hiss from his parted lips.

"Fuck," Clay swore.

Rose giggled and ran her hands over his wet shaft. "Now, that sounds like a deal to me," she teased, giving him back his words.

"On your knees, Honey," Clay ordered. Rose gave him a sexy little smirk and sunk to her knees, letting the water fall over her body. He palmed his cock, loving the way she seemed almost greedy to taste him.

"Open," he ordered. He didn't have to wait for Rose to comply. She leaned back on her heels and opened her mouth, looking up at him as if waiting for him to give her what she needed. Clay shoved his cock in past her willing lips and into the back of her throat. He loved the way she took over, letting him slide in and out of her mouth. Her tongue teasing the head every time he slipped out and then back into her hot mouth. He was so close but he didn't want to find his release down her throat. No, Clay wanted in her tight pussy.

Clay pulled his dick free from her mouth, loving the groan of displeasure she gave. "I know, Baby. I need in your pussy."

"Oh," Rose said, smiling up at him. Clay helped her to her feet and pressed her back up against the wall, lifting her so she could wrap her legs around his waist. His cock pushed through her wet folds allowing him to completely to sink into her body. Every time he took her felt like he was coming home and now was no different.

"You feel so fucking good, Honey," he breathed against her neck. Rose held onto his shoulders like he was her lifeline.

"You do too, Clay," she whimpered.

"This is going to be fast," he admitted. "I was so close when I was in your mouth, I almost came down your throat."

Rose groaned and nodded. "Please, Clay," she begged. Clay wasn't about to make her wait another minute.

"I've got you, Baby," he said. He pumped harder into her core and felt her tighten around his cock. She was close and he wanted Rose with him when he found his release. Clay flexed his fingers into her fleshy ass, kissing his way up to her mouth.

"I need you with me, Honey. I want you to touch yourself," he ordered. Rose seemed to hesitate at his command. "Rose," he warned. She closed her eyes as if trying to hide from him and nodded.

"Al-alright," she stuttered. Rose hesitantly snaked her hand down between their bodies and he could feel her fingers as they fumbled around to find her clit.

"You don't like to touch yourself?" he asked.

"I—I usually use a vibrator," she admitted. The thought of Rose getting herself off with a vibrator made him hot as hell. Clay moaned against her mouth and pumped furiously in and out of her pussy. He was so close.

"Tell me you're close," he growled.

"I am," she moaned. Rose's pussy clenched around his cock as she found her release and that was all Clay could stand. He pumped in and out of her body twice more and followed her over.

"Rose," he whispered her name like a prayer. He wanted to say so much more—tell her that he was falling for her. Hell, he had already fallen for her but saying those words out loud wasn't something she was ready to hear. Instead, he closed his eyes, pressing his forehead to hers. *I love you,* he thought, wishing he could say those words out loud. Someday, he would—when they were both ready to accept the truth.

ROSE

Rose stopped by her townhome to pick up her suitcase and a few things she needed for her trip and then called Ava to let her know that she would be stopping by. Her daughter-in-law would be her best ally in making Corbin listen to reason and right now, Rose needed all the help she could get. Ava told her that Corbin went into the office earlier that morning and as far as sulking went, he was going for the gold medal in that event. Rose almost wanted to laugh at just how far her son could take sulking when he was in the mood. Ava warned her that he wasn't in any better mood now that he had met Clay but Rose was done pussyfooting around. Corbin needed to hear from her how much his bad behavior and treatment towards Clay hurt her. It was time for her son to stop acting like a giant man child and luckily for her, Ava agreed. By the time she and her daughter-in-law came up with a plan, she had driven to the office and was ready to do her part.

Rose was waived through security and got on the

private elevator she and the boys used to access their penthouse office suites. She took a deep breath when the elevator stopped on the top floor, just before the doors opened. Rose knew what or who, in this case, would be waiting for her on the other side of the closed doors. Ava was supposed to call Corbin to warn him that his mom would be stopping by, giving him just enough time to meet her at the elevator.

The doors slid open and Corbin stared her down, arms crossed over his massive chest. Rose stepped out of the elevator and nodded to him, walking straight past him to her office.

"Mother," Corbin said, trailing behind her.

"Son," she returned.

"What are you doing here? Not only is it a weekend but you said you were taking next week off," Corbin reminded.

"It is and I did," Rose agreed. "I just needed a few things before I head off on my trip," she lied. She didn't need to stop by the office at all but if Corbin knew she was there to read him the riot act, she'd get nowhere.

"Trip," he asked. "Where are you going?"

"Austin, Texas," she said. "With Clay." Corbin's groan filled the empty office and she was happy that they were alone. She was a private person and spilling her dirty laundry for everyone in the office wasn't something she usually did.

"You just met the guy and now you're going on vacation with him?" Corbin questioned. Yeah, he wasn't going to like this next part but it was time for her to spell out her relationship with Clay for her son.

"I know you think things are going a little fast between Clay and me but it's none of your business." Corbin started to talk over her and she held up her hand, effectively stopping his tirade. "Before you say something stupid like I'm your mom and your business, let me remind you that I'm a grown woman and while I appreciate your concern, I won't let you bully me. I'm going on Clay's business trip with him and when we get back, I'm moving in with him."

"Moving in with him?" Corbin yelled. "Lower your voice, Corbin. I won't stand here and let you shout at me. Yes, I'm moving in with him. I told him that I'd move to his ranch and give this relationship a chance to play out."

"Are you going to marry him?" Corbin asked. That was a question she hadn't given much thought to. Clay hadn't asked and things between them were so new, marriage hadn't even crossed her mind.

"I haven't thought about marriage, Corbin. I'm enjoying the time I spend with him and whether you think so or not, I'm taking things slowly. I like Clay and he treats me well—that's all you need to know. My happiness should be enough for you."

Corbin exhaled and sat in one of the chairs she kept in front of her desk. "It is," he breathed. "I just don't want you to get hurt."

"I'm a big girl, Corbin. I think I can handle myself," she teased. Corbin refused to look at her and Rose knew that he wasn't telling her something. "What am I missing here, Son?" she asked.

"I didn't tell you because I didn't want to worry you.

My father reached out and he wants to meet with me."
Corbin still refused to look her in the eyes and Rose was
fine with that. She didn't want to have the reaction she
did about her ex. She thought she was past all the anger
of being left pregnant and alone at seventeen, but she
wasn't.

"Brock contacted you?" she whispered.

"Yeah," Corbin said. He stood, pacing in front of her
and Rose knew he was worried about telling her. She
didn't want to tell him that he shouldn't see the man
who left them both so long ago. It wasn't her place to
make that decision for him. "I think that's why I
responded to meeting Clay as I did. Brock reached out a
couple of days ago and I guess his message just set me
on edge. I'm sorry, Mom."

"Well, that's understandable, Corbin. You're a grown
man and he's never even bothered to get to know you. It
had to be a shock," Rose said, trying to be as understanding as possible.

"It was," he agreed. "He said that he has been
following my success and he found out about Brody and
wants to meet his grandson." Corbin slunk back into the
chair and looked up at her. "What the hell should I do,
Mom?"

"I can't tell you that, Son. What did Ava say?" Rose
asked.

"Nothing, really. She gets the whole, 'crazy father'
thing. Ava said it's up to me and I'm not sure what to do.
I don't know that I want him to be a part of my life.
What happens if I let him in, Brody gets to know him

and then he takes off again? I never had him in my life—why let him be a part of it now?"

"Again, I can't make that decision for you, Corbin. This is your decision to make, not mine." Rose said, sitting down in the chair next to him. Corbin shot her a sheepish grin and took her hand into his.

"It kind of is your decision, Mom. He's asked to see you too but he didn't have your contact information. He asked me to give you the message," Corbin almost whispered.

"Well, shit," Rose grumbled.

Corbin chuckled, "Mother," he teased. "Such a potty mouth." Rose tried not to curse; it was just who she was. In the office, she was constantly telling Aiden and Corbin to watch their language. Their wives had banned them from cursing around their homes with the kids listening on, so the boys had been using more swear words than normal lately. It took a lot for Rose to curse and the prospect of having to face her ex after more than thirty years pushed her over the edge of polite conversation.

Rose stood and nodded, "Thank you for delivering the message, Corbin. I don't have anything to say to Brock after all these years though."

Corbin stood, facing her. "I was hoping we could go together. You know, strength in numbers," he said. Corbin shrugged as if it was not a big deal but Rose could tell that it was to him.

"So, you've made up your mind then? You're going to see him?" Rose asked.

Corbin groaned and ran his hands through his

already unruly hair. "I don't know," he moaned. "You go on your trip and I'll think about what I want to do. I don't want to just jump into a decision and end up regretting it."

Corbin pulled her in for a quick hug, "Thanks, Mom. I'll try to give Clay a chance. Just make me a promise that if you need me, for any reason, you'll ask for my help."

"I promise," she said. "Thank you for giving Clay a chance."

"I said I'd try," Corbin corrected. "But, if he hurts you, I'll tear him apart."

Rose giggled, "I have a plane to catch. Walk me to the elevator?"

"Sure," Corbin said. "You tell Aiden you're going to Texas?"

"Not yet. I'll call him on my way home," Rose said. She pushed the button to call the elevator just as the doors opened and Aiden stepped off.

"I'm so glad you're still here," Aiden breathed. "I went by your house and Ava told me you were here and that Rose was stopping by."

"What's up, man?" Corbin asked. Rose knew that Aiden was a little high strung but this was next level, even for him.

"We have a problem," Aiden said. "The merger we've been working on these past few months—it might fall through." Rose knew the boys had been working non-stop to make sure the merger happened. It was the company's biggest deal so far and important to their companies future.

"Fuck," Corbin swore. "What the hell happened?"

"Our rival company happened," Aiden said.

"Newman and Sons?" Corbin asked.

"Yeah—apparently, one of the sons stuck his nose into our deal and now, the merger is being questioned," Aiden said.

"Which son?" Corbin growled. "If it's fucking Evan Newman, I'm going to tear him apart."

Rose put her hand on Corbin's arm. "You can't just go around threatening to tear people apart, Corbin."

Aiden chuckled, "It's Evan, and Rose is right. If you tear him apart, I won't be able to run this company while you're in prison. How about we sit down and come up with a solution that doesn't involve physical violence?" Aiden looked between Rose and Corbin and she hated that she was going to have to break the news about her trip to Aiden this way.

"I'm going out of town," Rose whispered.

"Wait—what?" Aiden questioned. "I thought you were just going to take some time off next week. Now, you're going away?"

Rose nodded, "Yes, sorry. I'm going to Texas with Clay."

"Can't you postpone that? We need you here, Mom. If this deal falls through, we could be facing some end of year layoffs. Please," Corbin begged.

Rose looked at Aiden and he shrugged and nodded. "He's right," Aiden agreed. "A lot is riding on this merger. We need you, Rose." She hated the idea of having to break the news to Clay that she wouldn't be going with him to Texas. He seemed so excited about their trip and even purchased her ticket last night before coming to bed.

"We wouldn't ask if it wasn't important, Rose," Aiden added. God, she couldn't say no to her boys, especially when they needed her help around the office. She knew how important this deal was for them and telling them no might send the whole merger down the toilet. She couldn't let that happen.

"Fine," she agreed. "I'll need to go home and break the news to Clay but I can be back here in a couple of hours to help." Aiden and Corbin both kissed her cheeks and she giggled. "But, when this merger goes through, I'm taking a week off—no questions asked."

"You got it," Aiden said. Rose stepped into the elevator and waved at them as the doors closed. She would have to run back to the ranch and break the news to Clay. Rose just hoped that he'd be okay with her backing out of their little trip—she'd just find a way to make it up to him, somehow.

CLAYTON

Clay spent four long days without Rose and he hated how much he missed her. It was unexpected and he found that instead of concentrating on the meetings and auctions he had to attend, he was daydreaming about the woman waiting for him back at home.

When Rose broke the news to him that she wasn't going to be able to go to Austin, he insisted that she stay out at his ranch while he was gone. She balked at the idea but then he told her it would make him hurry home faster knowing that a sexy as fuck, willing woman was waiting in his bed for him to return. He just didn't realize how true his words were because she was all he could think about while he was in Austin.

They talked on the phone every night like they were both high school sweethearts and she'd fill him in on what was going on around the ranch and how busy she was at work. The good news was that the merger had gone through, despite the hiccups and she was going to be able to take a few days off to spend with him. That news made Clay even more anxious to get home to Rose.

He dropped his bags in the front foyer and went into the kitchen, hoping to find Rose. Instead, he found his brother, Tyler. "Hey stranger. How was your trip?" Ty asked. He was rummaging through Clay's refrigerator and didn't stop building himself a monster sandwich to even look in his direction.

"Good," Clay said. "Where's Rose?"

Ty shrugged. "She hasn't been around."

"What?" Clay asked. "She told me she was staying here while I was away."

"Calm down, man. She was here last night but she said something about meeting her son about having to see someone. She seemed a little at odds. You know her son and I went to high school together, right?"

Clay sighed. He was tired of everyone reminding him about the age difference between him and Rose. It wasn't anyone else's business. "Yeah, I guessed that was the case. You and Corbin are about the same age. Does it really matter? I mean, does me being with an older woman bother you, Ty?"

Tyler stopped piling ham on his sandwich to look up at him. "No, why are you asking me that?"

"Because you keep bringing up our age difference. I mean, not outright but you drop subtle little hints and I want you to know that it doesn't bother me. Rose makes me happy."

"Then I'm happy for you," Ty admitted. "You deserve to be with someone who makes you smile, man. I see

135

the difference she's made in your life in just a few weeks. I think it's great, Clay."

"Thanks, Ty," Clay said. "I appreciate that." Rose came in through the side door and dropped her stuff on the bench next to the door. She looked as though she had a tough day and all Clay could think about was helping her to forget her bad day.

"Hey Honey," Clay said. He pulled her against his body and kissed her. "You look like you had a bad day."

"I did. But, it's better now that you're here. How was your trip home?" Rose asked, subtly changing the subject.

"Uneventful. How about you let me take you out to dinner?" he asked. Clay shot Ty a dirty look and laughed when his brother didn't seem to even notice. "My brother seems to have eaten us out of house and home." Clay teased

"Hey," Ty said around a mouthful of sandwich.

"I'd love to," Rose said. "But, we need to talk first." Clay looked her up and down, not missing the worry in her eyes.

"You're worrying me, Honey," he admitted. "What's up?"

"It's just something has come up and I need to fill you in." Rose looked down at her fidgeting hands and he took them into his own. "It's Corbin's father. Well, if that's what you'd call a man who created a new life with me and then just took off, not bothering to look back."

"I thought he wasn't a part of your or Corbin's life?" Clay questioned.

"He's not," she said. "He's never met my son." Ty

stopped eating his sandwich, setting it down on the counter and joining them in the foyer. Rose stopped talking and looked over at Ty.

"Really, Ty," Clay said. "You don't have anything better to do?"

"Nope," Tyler admitted.

"It's all right," Rose said. "This isn't something that's a secret, really."

"Thanks, Rose," Tyler said. "So, this guy just shows up out of nowhere and wants to see you and Corbin?"

"Yep," Rose said. "I met him when I was only fifteen. He was ten years older than me and I thought he was honestly my knight in shining armor. But, there's no such thing. Boy, was that a hard lesson to learn." Rose barked out her laugh and Clay wanted to protest, telling her that he'd ride in to save her from just about anything.

"What happened?" Tyler asked. Clay knew some of the story but he always wondered if there was more to it.

"I got pregnant," she admitted. "Brock was in my father's class at the university. My dad was a professor there and one night, he brought Brock home to introduce him to my mother. He was my dad's most promising student and he had such high hopes for Brock. One thing led to another and I started seeing Brock behind their backs. He convinced me that they wouldn't understand our relationship, given our age difference."

Tyler nodded, "Kind of like you and Clay," he said.

"Shut the fuck up, Ty," Clay growled.

"No, he's right. Maybe that's why I've had such a tough time with our age difference. But, in our case, I'm the one who's ten years older," Rose said.

"It's not the same," Clay said. "None of this has anything to do with us. I wouldn't have walked away from you, Rose—ever." He meant it too. They were past the point of pregnancy scares and doing the right thing but he knew with every fiber of his being that he would have stepped up if he was in that situation with Rose.

"I appreciate that, Clay. I know you aren't Brock but it took me a long time to get over being left like that. I told him I was pregnant and my parents threatened to have him arrested for having sex with a minor. Brock bolted leaving me pregnant and alone. My parents shut me out when I refused to have an abortion. They told me that if I chose not to terminate my pregnancy, they didn't want to have anything to do with me or my child. I just couldn't do it," Rose whispered. Clay pulled her into his body, needing contact with her.

"Of course you couldn't," Clay agreed. "You're such a good mom, Rose. I can see how much you love both Corbin and Aiden. Hell, you took in your son's best friend and raised him as your own. Not many people would do that."

"I do love those boys," she said. "I just had no idea how hard it was going to be—being a single mother, finishing high school and getting my diploma so I could get a crap job to keep us afloat. But, I did it. I'd do it all again, too. My son was worth every sacrifice I made."

"Why does your ex want to meet after all these years?" Clay asked.

"I have no idea, really," Rose admitted. "He got in touch with Corbin, saying he followed his career all these years and that he wanted to meet his grandson. Corbin's worried that if he lets that happen, he'll be setting Brody up for the same heartache he faced growing up without a father. I can't blame him, really."

"No one will blame Corbin if he decides not to meet with his father. But, why would you have to see him?"

"He asked to see me. Brock told Corbin that he didn't have any contact information for me and to give me the message. Truth is, I'm worried that Brock is up to no good but I'm just not sure what it is. I'd heard that he settled down and even got married. Last I heard, he and his wife had two kids and were happy. It hurt to hear that he found happiness with another woman, raising kids and having the family I should have had." Hearing Rose say that she wanted a family with another man made Clay half-crazy with jealousy.

"No family is perfect," Ty said. "You probably dodged a bullet when he walked away from you. Why would you want to be with a man who could do that to you?"

Rose shook her head, "I don't know," she whispered. "I guess it was the fantasy of it all—you know that perfect little family, cute house and white picket fence. The whole nine yards. I was a foolish girl. I had to grow up fast once Corbin got here and I never really looked back. I was too busy raising a kid."

"Are you going to see him," Clay asked.

"I don't know," Rose admitted. "I told Corbin that if he chose to see Brock, I'd go with him—you know for moral support. I don't really have any desire to have a reunion with the man who left me so easily."

"I get it," Ty said, still listening in. "What would you even say to him?"

"Okay Tyler, how about you take off and go check in at the barn," Clay ordered. Having his brother stick around for such a personal story probably made Rose feel uneasy. She was a very private person.

"Fine," Ty grumbled. "Good luck with your ex, Rose." Ty smirked at Clay and he honestly wanted to punch his brother.

"Thank you, Tyler," Rose said. Clay watched his brother leave and even locked the side door behind him.

"Sorry about him," Clay said.

"No, it's fine. I'm beginning to get used to Ty being around so much. It's his place too, really. He checked on me while you were gone—it was sweet the way he seemed to care."

"Well, he's never been accused of being sweet before. My brother has quite the reputation for being an ass when he wants to be," Clay said.

"Corbin said as much when he not so kindly reminded me that he and your brother went to school together. My son has a knack for pointing out the fact that I'm ancient compared to you." Clay nodded. He hated that most of their conversations came back to the fact that there was an age gap between them. He really wished people would quit reminding him and Rose about it. It felt like every step forward with Rose on the topic of their ages, led to two steps back.

"Does Corbin know if he's going to meet with Brock?" Clay asked.

"He decided this morning," Rose whispered.

"I'm assuming that you brought this up today because he agreed to see his father," Clay said. "And, you're going to go with him, aren't you?"

Rose nodded her head, "Yes," she said. "Corbin set up a dinner meeting for this coming Tuesday," Rose admitted.

"Would you have told me all of this if Corbin didn't agree to see him?" Clay asked. He wanted to believe that Rose would share all aspects of her life with him.

"Of course." Rose defiantly held her chin up as if challenging him to call her a liar. "You've been away, Clay. I found out about this the day you left for Texas and telling you over the phone didn't feel right. This was much too personal to just blurt out while you were hundreds of miles away. I wanted to tell you face to face. Heck, as soon as you walked through the door tonight, I spilled my guts to you." Rose was right and he felt like an ass for even asking her his question.

Clay pulled her against his body and Rose reluctantly let him. "I'm sorry, Honey. Forgive me for being such an ass?"

"You are an ass, Clay." Rose pouted and it was just about the cutest damn thing he'd ever seen. Clay dipped his hat back and kissed her full, pouty bottom lip, nipping it with his teeth.

"I missed you, Rose," he whispered against her mouth.

141

Rose sighed, "I missed you too," she said, seeming to give up some of her fight.

Clay smiled down at her, "How about you show me how much you missed me, Honey and I can make it up to you for being an ass?"

"You are going to have to do a whole lot of groveling to make up for being an ass, Clay," Rose teased. She freed herself from his arms, giggling and running down the hallway to the master bedroom. Clay reached for her, grabbing a handful of her shirt and pulled her back against his body.

"I want to play, Baby," he whispered into her ear. Rose's shiver told him she was up for a little fun too. He just hoped that his idea wouldn't fall flat. "Let me take you to my club," he asked.

"Your club?" Rose questioned.

"Yeah, I told you that I belong to a little BDSM club in town. I want to take you there and show you off a little. You up for that?" Clay asked. He felt as though he was holding his damn breath waiting for her to respond.

"People will see me?" she asked.

"Only if you want them too. I can get us a private room if you'd like to play behind closed doors." Rose didn't respond and Clay was about to give up. "Come on, Rose. Let me show you my world," he begged.

"Okay," she whispered. "We can try it."

Clay kissed her neck, "Thank you, Baby. If you don't like it or want to leave, just say the word."

"Walrus?" Rose asked. Clay was confused for a minute and then barked out his laugh.

"Yep, your safe word will work just fine," he agreed. "Now, go pick out your sexiest, skimpiest outfit and be ready to leave in twenty minutes," he ordered. Rose nodded and ran back to the bedroom. He was going to show Rose his world tonight—all of it and hopefully, she'd be ready for it. There would be no turning back now.

Clay loved the sexy little black dress that Rose picked out to wear for him. It hugged every one of her curves and he knew for a fact that she wasn't wearing panties or a bra underneath it. He had teased her to the point of almost having an orgasm on the ride over, letting his fingers leisurely slide through her drenched pussy. Clay loved her breathy sighs and gasps that told him she was close and her frustrated growls that erupted from her throat every time he removed his fingers.

By the time they got to the club, Rose was about ready to self-combust and completely relaxed—just how Clay wanted her. The more relaxed Rose was, the more things she'd be willing to try in the club.

"You remember your safe word?" he questioned.

"Walrus," Rose breathed. "Will I need to use it tonight?" she asked. Her voice still sounded raspy, needy, and completely sexy.

"Only if you don't like something we're trying. You have all the say here, Honey," Clay said. "We won't do anything you don't want to tonight."

"All right," she said.

"Good," Clay said. "Stay put," he ordered. He got out of the truck and rounded to the passenger side to grab her door for her. "Did I mention you look beautiful tonight?" he asked. He offered his hand to her and Rose took it, stepping down from his truck and straightened her dress.

"Yep," she breathed. "Just before you slipped your hand up my skirt and ran your fingers through my—" Rose didn't finish her sentence, smiling up at him. Clay liked that she was sometimes too shy to tell him the dirty parts of what she wanted. He considered it a challenge that she refused to say certain words. He hoped that more time in his playroom would have her saying all the dirty words.

She shot him a disgruntled look and he shrugged. "Don't expect me to apologize for the drive over here, Honey. I'm not one bit sorry." Rose shook her head at him and laughed.

"Fine," she said. "I'm sure you'll make it up to me."

"Oh—that's a promise, Baby." Clay pulled the door to the club opened and ushered Rose through. This wasn't his first time at the club but it was his first time bringing a woman with him. Usually, he hooked up with subs at the club and went back to his ranch alone. Not tonight. Tonight he was sure that he was entering the club with the prettiest woman there. All eyes were on him and Rose and he could just about feel her heart beating as she pressed her body up against his.

"You all right, Honey?" he whispered in her ear. Rose nodded and looked around the room. He could tell that the St. Andrews cross drew her attention. She had told him that she wanted to try it sometime and he took that as his cue to order one for his playroom. He was waiting to surprise Rose with the new addition to his room but tonight would be a perfect night to try it just to see if she liked it.

"You want to try the cross?" he questioned.

"Yes," she breathed. "Can we?" He nodded and looked around the room. The club wasn't very busy tonight and the smaller crowd would help get Rose over her shyness.

"Sure," he agreed. The cross was empty and Clay led Rose over to the corner of the room. "Strip," he commanded. Rose hesitated and he worried that she was reconsidering using her safe word. He wouldn't push but a part of him was secretly hoping that she'd agree to all his demands.

"I'm not wearing anything under this dress," she admitted.

Clay feigned shock and Rose rolled her eyes at him. "The point of this is for everyone to see my beautiful sub," he said. "Again, this is all your decision," Clay reminded.

"I want to do this," Rose said. He could almost see her resolve and courage and God, he was so proud of her. Rose stripped out of her dress standing completely bare in front of him. She shyly covered her breasts and Clay shook his head at her.

"I want to see all of you, Honey," he ordered. "I've got you." He blocked Rose from the few people who had gathered to watch her. Rose did as he asked and dropped her arms to her side. "Up against the cross,

Rose. I'm thinking I'd like to flog your sweet ass tonight so face the cross."

Rose quickly turned and pressed her body up against the wooden cross, gifting him with a view of her glorious ass. "Perfect, Honey," he said slapping her fleshy globe. Clay worked quickly to secure her wrists and ankles, leaving Rose completely vulnerable and open for him to play with. Clay grabbed a flogger from the rack and ran the soft leather tip up her thighs, teasing every inch of her. Clay's cock protested that it had to wait for its turn.

"You're perfect, Honey," he said. Clay ran the flogger over her ass, giving it a sharp slap that rang through the playroom. They had drawn quite a crowd but Rose had no clue since she was facing away from the club members who were looking on. He gave her a few more sharp slaps with the flogger, loving her breathy little sighs and moans. Rose strained against her bindings and Clay was sure that he had found the perfect woman for himself. He dipped the tip of the flogger between her parted thighs again and rubbed it through her wet folds. Rose moaned and tried to thrust back, needing the release that he had been withholding from her.

"Please, Clay," she begged.

"Please, Sir," he reminded.

"Sir, I need to come," she cried.

"Fuck," Clay heard a man swore and turned to find Rose's very pissed off hulk of a son standing behind him. "What the fuck are you doing to my mother?" Corbin shouted over the hum of the crowd.

"Shit," Clay cursed. He covered Rose's body with his own.

"Oh my God," Rose whispered. "My son is here?"

"Yeah, Honey. I'm so sorry. I didn't know that he's a member here," Clay whispered into her ear. "Could you maybe give her some privacy to slip her dress back on?" he asked Corbin.

"Sure," Corbin said. "And then how about you meet me outside so I can beat the shit out of you?" Corbin turned to make his way back through the crowd. He took the hand of a pretty woman who Clay assumed was his wife, Avalon. He needed to get Rose dressed and grovel for her to forgive him and then he'd face her son.

Clay undid her bindings and found her dress, helping her back into it and shielding her body from the onlookers. "You have to know I didn't know he comes here, Rose. I'm so sorry. I didn't plan any of this."

"Of course you didn't," Rose said. "I'm sorry that he saw me like that but I won't apologize for what we're doing here. Let's go sort this out." Clay followed Rose out of the club and they found Corbin and his wife standing by his pick-up.

"I guess he figured out which truck is mine," Clay grumbled.

"Well, you do have your ranch's logo on the side of your truck," Rose said.

Corbin started for them and Rose stood between him and Clay. "Move Mom," Corbin shouted.

"No," she yelled back. "You will not lay a finger on Clay. This wasn't his fault. I wanted this, Corbin." Her son took a step back from her as if Rose slapped him.

"You wanted this?" he yelled. "You wanted to be taken into a BDSM club and have your ass flogged in front of all of those people?" Ava caught up to Corbin and smiled at Rose.

"I'm Ava," she said, nodding to Clay. "I've heard a lot about you, Clay."

"Sorry to have to meet like this," Clay said.

Ava smiled and nodded at Clay and then turned to face her very pissed off husband. "Honey, you're forgetting that I like to be taken to a BDSM club and have you flog my ass. You didn't invent kink," Ava said. "What your mom was doing in there was completely normal and none of your business." God love Ava, she seemed to be the voice of reason when it came to calming Corbin.

"But," Corbin tried to argue. Ava cocked her eyebrow at him and magically silenced him.

"Not our business," she repeated. "It was good to meet you, Clay," Ava said. She pulled Rose in for a quick hug and grabbed Corbin's hand. "Time to head home," Ava insisted. Corbin reluctantly followed his wife back to his SUV and slid into the driver's seat after helping her into the vehicle. He never took his eyes off Clay and if looks could kill, he'd be dead a few times over.

"Well, that was a shit show," Clay whispered.

"I'm sorry," Rose said. "Are we good?"

"I should be the one asking you that, Honey," Clay said. He wrapped an arm around Rose and walked her to his truck.

"We're good," she promised. "Now, take me home and finish what you started," she said.

"You sure?" Clay questioned. "We can just call it a night if you'd rather."

"Nope," Rose said, smiling up at him. "I'd like to see how close you can get to working me up to use my safe word." Clay chuckled and started his truck.

"Well, all right then," he said.

ROSE

The next morning, Rose headed into the office early hoping to avoid another scene with Corbin. Unfortunately, he and Aiden were both waiting for her at her desk.

"Well, you two are early birds this morning. Everything all right?" Rose wasn't going to bring up the club unless Corbin did first. As far as she was concerned, that was behind them and didn't need to be rehashed.

"You're here awfully early yourself," Aiden taunted. She could tell from the shit-eating grin he wore that Corbin had filled him in already. "Especially after the eventful night you had last night."

"Oh—" Rose looked between Aiden and Corbin as if daring either of them to call her out for being at the club. "What events are you referring to, Aiden?" she questioned already knowing the answer.

"Cut the shit, Mom," Corbin growled. "You know exactly what he's talking about. What the fuck were you thinking?"

"I was thinking that I wanted a fun night out with a man that I care deeply for. I'm also thinking that what I do with my time and whom I do it with is none of your damn business," she shouted, pointing her finger into her son's massive chest. "We've already been over this, Corbin."

Aiden chuckled and shook his head. "What so funny?" Rose asked.

"You and your caveman son," Aiden said. "And, for the record, you are correct—it's none of our business but you have to understand that Corbin and I both go there with the girls. Our wives are both into kink," Aiden said, bobbing his eyebrows at her. Rose made a disgusted sound in the back of her throat.

"See, now you know how I feel," Corbin chimed in. "I had to see parts of you that I didn't ever want to see, Mom."

"Oh, don't be so dramatic, Corbin," Rose chided. "You'll be fine. You have plenty of money—why not go see a therapist and tell him how your mother failed you."

"Now who's being dramatic, Mother?" Corbin asked.

"Before this gets into a shouting match and takes up the rest of our already busy day," Aiden said. "How about we work out a schedule so this doesn't happen again?" "A schedule?" Rose asked.

"Yes," Aiden said. "Corbin and I have worked out a schedule for when we can go to the club so Ava and Zara don't have to feel embarrassed if the other just happens to pop up—like what happened with you and

Lug Head here." Corbin shot daggers at Aiden and Rose quickly piped up.

"A schedule sounds perfect," she said. "What nights do you guys have?"

"I have Tuesdays with Zara. It's a standing date and we have a regular babysitter that watches the kids," Aiden said.

"Ava and I take Saturdays. It's the only day that neither of us is crazy with work," Corbin said.

"Um, okay," Rose tried to think of Clay's schedule. "How about if I take Fridays?" she asked.

"Sounds good," Aiden agreed. "See this wasn't so hard."

"Fine," Corbin grumbled. "And, it was easy for you because you didn't have to see mom naked, strapped to the cross, and getting her ass flogged."

"Not cool, Man. Now I won't be able to shake that image from my brain. Not cool at all," Aiden mumbled as he made his way to his office.

"We good?" Rose asked her son.

"Yep," he said. Rose noticed how he refused to look her in the eyes and worried that he had just lied to her. "No," he corrected. "But, we will be. I just need a little time and space, Mom." Rose nodded. That wasn't going to be a problem for her because honestly, she felt the same way. Corbin walked back to his office and shut the door and Rose slunk into her office chair. She was exhausted and it was only eight in the morning. Yeah, it was going to be a hell of a long day.

※

It had been a day since their incredibly awkward conversation about her son finding her in the club. Rose had laid low and Corbin seemed to forget the whole thing. At least, that was what she was hoping. Tonight, they were going to meet up with Corbin's biological father and she could tell he was nervous about the meeting. He had spent most of his day locked away in his office while Aiden and Rose attended meeting after meeting, putting out small fires as they popped up.

They drove in complete silence to the meeting and when they got to the restaurant, Corbin grabbed her hand and squeezed it; a telltale sign that her son was just as nervous about this dinner meeting with her ex as she was.

"We'll be fine," she whispered. Honestly, she worried that it was a total lie. Nothing about seeing the man who left her pregnant and alone to raise her son felt "fine" to her. She promised Corbin that she'd be by his side for the meeting and that was exactly what she planned to do.

Clay had offered to join them but that would be the last thing her son would want. He had promised to give Clay a chance but they were still taking baby steps in their relationship. Plus, she didn't want Clay to be tainted by the bad choices of her past. Corbin's biological father was one of her worst choices. The only good thing that came out of their relationship was her son. She needed to remember that when she looked into her ex's eyes and felt only contempt.

They got into the little Italian restaurant that she knew was her son's favorite and she looked around, trying to see if she could spot Brock after all these years. He was sitting in a corner booth in a dark corner and stood to wave them over as soon as he saw them.

"He's over there," Rose whispered to her son. She had forgotten how much Corbin resembled his father. He got his size from Brock and his good looks. She remembered just how much she wanted to be with him when she was younger but now, when she looked him over, all Rose felt was sadness. Not for herself. More for her son who had to miss out on having a father in his life. She tried to fill the voids for him but a boy needed a male influence no matter how good she got at throwing a baseball.

"Rose," Brock said. He looked unsure of what to do next. She could tell that he wanted to hug her but that was unacceptable.

"Brock," she said. Rose nodded at him and crossed her arms over her chest, letting him know in no uncertain terms that touching her was not an option. "This is my son, Corbin," she said. Sure, she was hitting a little below the belt, introducing him that way but she didn't care.

"Corbin," Brock said, holding out his hand. Corbin shook his hand and nodded.

"Good to meet you," he said. Corbin ushered her into the opposite side of the booth from where her ex was sitting and slid in next to her.

"This is a nice little place," Brock said. Rose could tell he was trying to break the ice but exchanging pleasantries wasn't why they were there.

"Why did you ask to meet with us, Brock?" she asked, getting right down to business.

"Yes, I guess we'll just get right to it then," Brock breathed. "I wanted to meet my son." He simply said it as if that would explain everything after all these years.

"Well, that explains everything," Rose grumbled. "You just woke up one day and decided it was time? He's thirty-three years old, Brock. It wasn't time to meet him when he was born? How about when he was ten and had to have his appendix out and was scared to death. Maybe when he graduated from high school or college —wouldn't that have been the right time? Instead, you waited until he was grown and had a multi-billion dollar company under his belt and then you crawl out from whatever rock you were hiding under."

"Mom," Corbin whispered.

"Maybe this was a mistake," Brock said. "I shouldn't have asked you to join us."

"She's the only reason I'm here," Corbin said. "If my mother didn't agree to come with me, this meeting wouldn't be happening. So, I'll ask you one last time before we leave. Why did you want to see us?" Corbin stared Brock down and Rose had never felt prouder of her son.

Brock heaved out a sigh and shook his head. "I have cancer," he said. "I'm dying."

Corbin sat back in the booth and looked Brock over. "You look pretty healthy to me," he countered.

"I've been doing my chemo but the doctors said that this period of feeling good won't last," Brock said.

"Unless I can get a bone marrow transplant, I won't make it another six months."

Rose barked out her laugh. "Ah—now we're getting somewhere. You wanted to meet your biological son to see if you two are a match. Am I getting it right, Brock?"

"No," he protested. "I wanted to meet him to tell him that I don't have long to live."

"Then why bring up the whole bone marrow topic," Rose challenged.

"Because it's the truth. A bone marrow donor match is the only way I'll beat this thing," Brock admitted.

"And you think I'll be a match?" Corbin asked. Rose hated that her son was being put in this situation. He had such a big heart; Corbin would go out of his way to help just about anyone if it were within his power. She just hoped he didn't overlook the big picture in his hurry to help a man who probably wouldn't return the favor if the shoe were on the other foot.

"The doctors told me that a blood relative would be my best match. My younger kids weren't matches. You or your son might be though," Brock said.

"No fucking way are you taking anything from my son," Corbin said. He stood and pulled Rose with him out of the booth. "I'll get tested but my son will not be. If I'm a match, I'll donate bone marrow to you. But, that's it. You won't contact my mother or me again —ever."

"But," Brock stuttered. He stood and Corbin towered over him.

"But nothing, Brock," he shouted. "There is no room for argument. You didn't come here looking for a relationship with me or to ask forgiveness from the woman you walked away from. What type of man walks away from the woman carrying his child? As a father now myself, I can tell you that's a pretty unforgivable offense. You don't deserve anything from me but I wouldn't be able to live with the fact that I didn't at least get tested. So, I will. But, that's where this ends. Take it or leave it." Rose wrapped her arm around Corbin worried that if Brock said the wrong thing, her son would do what she so desperately wanted to and punch the asshole.

"I'll take it," Brock said. He sat back down in the booth and Corbin didn't say another word. He nodded and turned to leave.

"My attorney will be in touch with the results," Corbin said over his shoulder. "If you have any questions, you can go through my team. We won't be meeting again face to face—ever." He held the door open for Rose and she walked out into the parking lot, blinking against the sun.

"I'm sorry, Son," she whispered, taking Corbin's offered hand.

"Not your fault, Mom," he said. "We're better off without him."

"You can say that now because you don't know what your life could have been like if he had stuck around. You missed out on a father who would have taken you to little league games, taught you to ride a bike, thrown the football with you, and taught you about girls," Rose said.

"Yeah, I did miss out on a father who wanted to

teach me those things but I had you, Mom. You did all those things with me. You taught me how to throw a knuckleball and swing a bat. You were the one who taught me how to slow dance with a girl for my seventh-grade dance, so I wouldn't fuck things up too bad. You were the one who sat in the stadium every Friday night during high school to cheer me on when I played football. I've never thanked you for all of that," Corbin said. He opened the car door for her and she slid into her seat, happy for the reprieve as Corbin rounded the front of the car and got into the driver's seat. Rose fought to keep her tears at bay, not wanting to let the emotions of the day overcome her but each passing moment was proving harder and harder to do that.

"Shit, Mom—don't cry," Corbin groaned as she wiped her hot tears from her face.

"It's been a long week," Rose defended. "And, hearing you say nice things was just—well, it was just nice. But son, don't shut Brock out of your life just to spare my feelings. If you want to have a relationship with him, don't let my feelings towards him dissuade you."

Corbin reached across the center console and took her hand into his. "I've made my decision, Mom. It was my own and I won't be changing my mind. I appreciate what you said, though. I'll get tested and then we'll go from there. But, I won't let that man into my life or my son's life. He's just not worth it. Besides, Brody already has the best fucking grandma in the world, what more could the kid want?" Corbin teased.

"I can still throw a mean knuckleball and I'm an excellent cheerleader. Thanks, Son," Rose said.

"Anytime, Mom. Now, let's get something to eat, I'm starving. That was the worst dinner meeting I've ever had." Rose checked her watch and nodded.

"Let me text Clay and tell him that I'm staying at my townhome tonight. I have a feeling he'll be in bed by the time I finally get back to the ranch and I could use a night to myself to decompress," she said.

Corbin chuckled and started his car. "Just as long as he doesn't think I'm the one keeping you from him. I'm trying to make up for my bad behavior."

"Yeah, that's probably a good idea—you are on thin ice, Corbin," she teased.

ROSE

Two Weeks Later

Rose sat down at Clay's big mahogany desk. His whole office was so masculine from the trophy antlers and stuffed deer heads adorning the wood-paneled wall down to the fishing gear he kept stowed in the corner. Of course, her favorite piece in the room was the riding saddle that he perched in the corner on the coffee table. Clay had originally kept the saddle in his playroom but moved it to his office when he had the St. Andrews cross installed, giving them more room to play. She loved that saddle and everything Clay had done to her while she straddled it their second night together. She smiled and shook her head at the way she felt her whole body blush at just the memory of him commanding her every need.

Clay had gone out to the main barn to check on a horse who was foaling and if she hurried she could get Aiden his contracts before the pony was born. Rose wanted to see the little guy enter the world. For a city girl, she was finding every nuance of the ranch fascinating. Clay told her she'd be an old farm hand before long but she wasn't sure she'd ever get used to life on his ranch.

Rose opened Clay's laptop that he let her borrow and typed in the password he had shared with her. A cute picture of him and Paisley popped up on his main screen that made her smile. Rose hoped that at some point Clay's teenage daughter wouldn't seem to hate her so much. She understood how the girl felt. She was just thirteen years old and a part of her probably lived under the deluded fantasy that her parents would get back together.

Abilene seemed to be warming up to her—slowly. Rose couldn't see her and Clay getting back together. He had told her time and again that he and his ex-wife were just friends determined to make the whole co-parenting thing work for Paisley's sake. Abi was finally letting Clay have some time with Paisley and a part of Rose felt guilty every time the teen stared her down when Clay and Abi handed her off. It was crazy that Paisley blamed Rose for her parents split, especially since they had been divorced for almost five years now. She hadn't been a teenager for a damn long time but she could remember the hormones she had to deal with daily and she worried that her relationship with Paisley might never improve. Teen girls were irrational and emotional and that was the case on their best days.

Rose's phone chimed and she pulled it from her pocket but was sure she knew exactly who it was. Aiden was almost as impatient as Corbin; especially when it came to business contracts. "Yes, Aiden," she answered.

"Were you able to find a laptop?" he asked. "If not, I'd be happy to send yours over via courier." Rose was regretting leaving her laptop at work for her week "off". She had finally decided to take some much-needed vacation days and spend them with Clay around his ranch. In a grand gesture, she told the boys that she was leaving her laptop in her desk, locking the drawer and throwing away the key. Her freedom lasted all of one day before Aiden was calling her and begging her to help him find some files. When she asked him if they could wait until next week he just about had a meltdown.

"I'm not sure if I should find your offer sweet and charming or bossy and overbearing," Rose teased him. "I love you like you're my son, Aiden. You know how I feel about you but if you don't give me a little faith, my feelings will be hurt."

"You didn't answer my question," he said. "Do you need me to send your laptop to you?"

"No," she breathed. "Clay is letting me borrow his."

"So, I can expect my files?" Aiden asked.

"Yes, Aiden," she moaned. "I'm working on them now. You know what would help me get them to you faster?" she asked.

"Name it," he said.

"You leaving me alone to do my job and quit micro-managing me. I am, after all, on vacation," Rose chided.

Aiden chuckled into the other end of the phone and she knew that asking Aiden to back off was like asking a cheetah to change its spots. Relaxing and letting someone else take some of his load wasn't in his wheelhouse.

"I'll be here in my office watching for the files to come through, Rose," he said. "Talk soon." He ended his call and she shook her head at her cell phone.

"Bossy," she whispered, returning her attention to Clay's laptop. Rose logged into the companies secure website and pulled up her files. This deal was going to be huge for the company and Corbin and Aiden had been on edge for months now. She was looking forward to the deal being done and the contracts signed. They would all be able to breathe a little easier once this deal was behind them. Rose attached the contracts onto an email and hit send, smiling from ear to ear like a loon.

"Done," she said. "Now, time for some wine." She planned on making Clay her famous buttered chicken for dinner and then she was hoping he'd take her to his playroom for some fun. She missed going to the club with him but a promise was a promise. Corbin made her swear on her grandson's life that she'd not show her face in the club he and his wife frequented unless it was her appointed night. Clay had been working so many long hours around the ranch that asking him to take her to the club on a Friday evening, after he had worked all day, didn't seem fair. Still, it was an easy promise to keep once Clay took her to her favorite room in the house. His secret playroom was equipped for more pleasure than she could handle.

Rose logged out of the company's website and was just about to turn off Clay's laptop when a private message popped up on the screen. She was going to downsize it until she read who it was sent by—Clay's ex-wife Abilene. Rose wondered why she wouldn't just contact him by his cell and worried that Clay wasn't getting his messages out in the barn. Abi had Paisley and Rose worried that something might have happened and she'd need to get the message to Clay. Plus, there was that small part of her that was curious about the message. She trusted Clay completely but she was only human and as her son liked to point out—nosey.

Rose sat back in Clay's big leather office chair and studied the computer screen. "Shit," she whispered to herself. "I really shouldn't do this," she huffed. Rose ran her finger over the keyboard and opened the message; sitting forward to read Abi's PM.

Hey—we still on for Saturday night? I can't wait to see you again. Honestly, last Tuesday was one of the best nights of my life. Don't worry, I will keep this our little secret until you can figure out how to get rid of Rose.

Rose read the message four more times, trying to figure out what it meant exactly. Clay was seeing his ex? That just couldn't be. Rose pulled her cell phone from her pocket and scrolled through her apps, trying to find her calendar with her shaky fingers. She wiped the hot tears that were freely falling down her cheeks and pulled up her schedule from last Tuesday. She and Clay had spent almost every evening together since they met. Hell, she was beginning to forget what her little town-home even looked like since they usually stayed at his ranch. It was easier that way with his early mornings and late nights. Rose had even accepted his offer of moving in with him so why would he start seeing his ex-wife again?

She looked over the entire day from last Tuesday, remembering each hour as if it had just happened yesterday. They had meeting after meeting at work that day and then she and Corbin met her ex for their dinner meeting. It turned out to be a late-night and rather than driving back out to the ranch and waking Clay, she spent the night at her townhouse. That night she realized that missing Clay sucked and it wasn't something she wanted to do often.

The fact remained, he could have spent the night with his ex-wife and Rose would have never known. The question was, would Clay do that to her? He told her he was falling for her but they hadn't given each other the words. There were no grand sweeping declarations of love made yet, although he did ask her to move in with him. He was a free man and ten years her junior. If he was seeing his ex, she wanted to know. It was going to hurt like hell to walk away from him but she'd never been with a man who could sneak around behind her back and cheat on her. Clay had her heart, whether he knew that fact or not but Rose still had a death grip on her pride—for now.

Rose closed the laptop and neatly tucked everything back into place, sliding his office chair back under his desk. She turned off the lights to his office and padded to the kitchen. She'd wait for him to come back from the barn and then she'd confront him about Abi's message. She looked around the spacious room and sobbed at the thought of confronting him. Rose wasn't a coward but having to face the man she loved and ask him such a darkly disturbing question scared the crap out of her. She ran through the scenarios of what she'd say and how she would respond to his denials. Rose even considered finding the bottle of wine she had been saving for their dinner but thought twice about drinking before their conversation.

Fifteen minutes passed and it felt as if it had been hours. With every passing minute, Rose's nerve deteriorated and she felt the strength she prided herself for, slowly slipping away. She found her purse and her car keys, deciding that what she needed was time to think and she couldn't do that at Clay's ranch. She needed to be at her townhome, in her own space, so she could get her head on straight. Then, she'd find a way to face Clay when she was stronger and calmer.

Rose was just about to her car when Clay rounded the corner into the garage. He parked his truck in its bay and looked over at her. He jumped down out of the cab of his pick-up and started towards her. Rose could see that he was confused and why wouldn't he be? They had plans tonight. She was going to make them a nice dinner but Rose couldn't think about any of that now. Self-perseverance kicked in and she quickly hopped into the driver's seat of the car and turned on the engine. She chanced one last look over at Clay and instantly regretted it. He was shouting her name and before he could run over to her car, she pulled out of the garage. Rose didn't bother to look back again—she knew what she'd find—him staring back at her and that would be more than she could take. Clay's disappointment was going to tear her heart out and she needed to keep it together long enough to get back to her place. Then, Rose could fall apart and figure out how to pick up the pieces and put herself back together again. That's how she raised her son and Aiden on her own. It's who she was and what she did—broken heart be damned.

CLAYTON

Clay watched as Rose sped out of his garage and down the long drive that led away from him. Where the hell was she running to? They were supposed to have a nice romantic dinner together. He had planned on taking her to his playroom and introducing her to a few new toys he had gotten for her. Then, he planned on telling Rose that he was more than falling for her. He had fallen in love with her and it was about time he gave her the words that were always on the tip of his tongue every time she gave him her submission and the gift of her body. She was so perfect for him and it was past damn time that he told her that.

Clay had waited so long to find someone who wanted the same things he did. He struggled with his dominance, worried that he'd never find a woman who'd want him for who he truly was. His ex-wife never liked his dominant nature. Hell, it's what ended up destroying their marriage. He spent countless nights at the club, sating himself with women who tried to be what he needed but they only got a glimpse of who he was. He was too demanding and ended up scaring off most of the women who promised to be his perfect playmate.

He looked through the house for any sign of what had spooked Rose enough to make her run away as she had. The kitchen was spotless and there were no signs of her making dinner. Maybe she had decided to order out and was just going to pick it up but that wouldn't explain the pain he saw in her eyes when she looked at him.

"This is ridiculous," he breathed. Clay pulled his cell phone from his jeans and tried to call Rose. If she was upset about something he needed to know what it was so he could fix it. His call went straight to voicemail and he cursed under his breath. Rose's cheery voice prompted him to leave her a message and by the time the beep sounded, he was about ready to get back into his damn truck and go looking for her.

"Rose," he growled. "Where the fuck are you?" Clay took a deep breath, trying to reign in his anger. "Listen, just call me and let me know that you are okay. Talk to me, tell me what's wrong. Whatever it is, we'll figure it out together but don't shut me out." Clay ended the call and tossed his cell onto the kitchen counter.

He tried to remember what Rose had planned to do before he left for the barn. She had asked him if she could use his laptop and he, of course, told her yes. Clay walked back through the house to his office and found it just like he found the kitchen—everything in its place and neat as a pin. He flicked on the lights and looked around, walking over to sit behind his desk. He opened his laptop and waited for it to boot up. As soon as it did, he saw that he had a private message from Abi and he wondered why she hadn't just called his cell. He opened the message worried that something was wrong with Paisley and his service was down while he was down in the barn.

He read and re-read the message a least a half dozen times, trying to figure out what his ex's message meant. Maybe she had sent it by mistake. She was seeing some guy, at least that was what Paisley had told her. Maybe Abi sent Clay the message instead of her new boyfriend.

"Shit," he mumbled. "She must have read this." That would explain why Rose sped out of there like her ass was on fire. It would also explain the eye daggers she was shooting him on her way out. The only way he was going to work this out with Rose was to figure out why Abi had sent him the message in the first place.

He walked back to the kitchen to find his cell. He pulled up Abi's number and called her. She answered on the third ring. "Clay," she said.

"Abi," he returned. Their relationship had always remained cordial but she was always short and to the point with him. "Want to tell me what your message was all about?" His question sounded more like an acquisition and he took a breath and let it out, releasing some of his pent up anger. "Sorry," he said. "I'm just a little on edge."

"No problem." Abi let the silence fill the call and he worried she wasn't going to answer his question. "Um, what message? I just looked through my texts with you and I haven't sent you any new messages."

"It wasn't through text. It came through on my computer as a private message," he said. "Hold on." Clay went back to his office and opened his laptop. As soon as it booted up he copied and pasted the message to send back to Abi. "I just texted you the message you sent me."

Again, there was silence on Abi's end and he felt like he was holding his damn breath. He needed answers. Hell, he needed to find Rose and tell her that Abi's message wasn't real. He needed to tell her he'd never cheat on her. He was in love with Rose and planned on spending the rest of his life with her but he didn't tell her that. Instead, he was taking things slow and letting her get used to the newness of their relationship. It's what she had asked him for and instead of following his gut instincts, he allowed her to set the pace. Sure, it had only been two months since they met at the bar, on their birthdays, but it had felt like a lifetime that he had known Rose.

"What the hell?" Abi breathed. "I didn't send this to you, Clay."

"Well, whoever you were trying to send it to never got it, Abi and it's messed things up with Rose and me," he said.

"I didn't send this message at all, Clay. Not to you or anyone else. But, I have a sneaky feeling I know who did. Paisley was using my laptop tonight. She said that she left her charger at your place and her battery died. I think our daughter intended for Rose to find that

message. I'm sorry, Clay. I know she's become important to you."

"Fuck," he swore. "I'm in love with Rose," he whispered. "Why would Paisley do this? I know she isn't
Rose's biggest fan but to hurt her like this is just plain
mean. Put her on the phone," he ordered. "I want to talk
to her."

Abi barked out her laugh. "You think that yelling at
our thirteen-year-old daughter is going to make things
any better, Clay? How about I sit her down and try to
figure this out and you work things out with Rose.
Then, we can all sit down and get to the bottom of why
Paisley is acting out like this."

Abi was right—shouting at Paisley would get him
nowhere. All he wanted to do was find Rose and explain
that he would never cheat on her and that this whole
thing was the evil plan of one very grounded thirteen-
year-old girl.

"Fine," he agreed. "But, she's grounded."

"Agreed," Abi said. "And Clay—good luck with Rose.
I know I acted like an ass when I first met her, but I
hope everything works out between the two of you. I'm
happy that you've found someone." Abi ended the call.

"Thanks," Clay whispered. "Me too."

Clay spent the better part of the night trying to track
down Rose. He went by her townhome and pounded
on her door only to have it answered by her very angry
hulk of a son. Corbin wasn't too happy to see him and

from the look in his eyes, about ready to tear him apart.

Clay held up his hands, "Before you go and do something you might regret," he warned.

"Oh, I won't regret a single second of pounding you into a pulp for hurting my mother, Clay," Corbin said.

"I didn't do anything to hurt Rose," Clay defended. "The message was a fake."

"Bullshit," Corbin accused. "You were double-timing my mother and now, you are covering your tracks to save your sorry ass." Corbin was a scary site angry but Clay wouldn't back down, not even if the guy didn't believe him. What did he have to lose if Rose wouldn't give him a second chance?

"It was from my daughter, Paisley," Clay said.

"Your daughter?" Corbin questioned. "I thought the message was from your ex-wife."

"You know that my thirteen-year-old daughter doesn't much care for me seeing your mom," Clay admitted. "My ex didn't send me that message—my teenage daughter did. I'm betting she was hoping that Rose would see it and take off."

"Well, mission accomplished," Corbin said. "My mother doesn't want to see you, Clay. Do you have any idea how badly seeing that message hurt her?"

"Is she all right?" Clay asked. God, the thought of Rose hurting just about tore his damn heart out. "Is she here? I just want to explain."

"I think it would be best for you to give her some time, man," Corbin said. "Let her decide for herself if she thinks you're worth all of this trouble."

"Trouble?" Clay asked. "What the fuck does that mean?" He took a step towards Corbin, going toe to toe with the big guy. He wouldn't back down from whatever threat Corbin posed—Rose wasn't someone he was willing to let go of.

"It means that you've upset my mother and I won't allow you to do it again," Corbin growled.

"And, I told you that message was a fake. I would never hurt your mother," Clay challenged.

"What's stopping your daughter from doing something like this again? What's stopping her from hurting my mother?" Corbin made a good point. Clay couldn't stop Paisley from going after Rose again to hurt her. Sure, this time it was words that did the damage but what would stop her from taking things to the next level? He and Abi were going to have their work cut out with her but he'd make sure Paisley didn't hurt Rose ever again.

"My ex and I are going to have to work through this with our daughter. I won't stand for Paisley hurting Rose again—ever. You just need to believe that," Clay begged.

"I don't need to believe anything, Clay," Corbin said. "My mother's off-limits."

"I appreciate you wanting to protect your mom, Corbin. But, I need the chance to explain what happened. I need to tell her that I've fallen in love with her," Clay almost whispered. He couldn't believe that he was standing on Rose's front porch telling her grown son that he was in love with her. He pictured saying those words out loud going so differently. Sharing his feelings with Corbin wasn't part of that picture. Clay watched as Corbin ducked his head back behind the door. He could hear him whispering, or what he assumed was Corbin's attempt at a whisper. The man honestly had one volume.

"Hold on," Corbin said. He shut the door but Clay could still hear Corbin's voice and who he assumed to be Rose's voice on the other side of the door. After a few minutes of what sounded like a heated debate, Rose opened the door, Corbin standing behind her. Judging from the angry expression he wore; he had lost the fight and reluctantly gave Rose her way.

"Rose," Clay said. She had fresh tears in her eyes and Clay hated that he was the person who made her cry. If it had been someone else who made Rose cry, he'd want to tear that person apart.

"Clay," she whispered, raising her chin defiantly.

"I'm so sorry," he said. "Paisley sent that message, not Abi. Nothing is going on with us. Hell, there's no one else—just you. Tell me you believe me, Rose," he begged.

She held up her hand, stopping him from saying another word, and Clay worried she was going to tell him to leave. "What did you just tell Corbin?" she asked.

"Corbin?" he asked. Clay thought back over what he and Corbin had just discussed and when he realized what she was asking, he couldn't hide his smile.

"Oh, you mean that I love you?" Clay asked. Rose sobbed and covered her mouth with her shaking hand.

"Yeah," she said. "That."

"I do, Rose. I have since the first night I met you. I just needed to get up the nerve to tell you." Clay looked over Rose's shoulder to where Corbin stood, still listening to their private conversation. "Mind giving us a few minutes?" Clay asked.

Corbin shook his head, "That's up to my mom," he said.

"I'm fine, Corbin," Rose said. "Maybe just go to the kitchen and make a snack or something."

"All right," Corbin grumbled. "But, there better be ice cream in your freezer."

Rose waited until her son had disappeared to the back of her house and turned back to face Clay down. "I can't do this," she whispered. "Not now."

"If you want to talk privately, we can go back to my ranch," he offered.

"This has nothing to do with Corbin being here or our lack of privacy. I can't do this at all, Clay."

"Wait, what?" he asked. Here he had just poured out his heart and soul for the woman he loved and she wasn't giving him an inch. "Please, believe me, Rose. I haven't been cheating on you with Abi or anyone else for that matter."

"I do believe that, Clay. At first, I had my doubts. You and Abi have a history and a child together. That's a pretty strong bond and I believed you might want another chance at being a family with her. But, I believe that Paisley was the one who sent the email. Your daughter doesn't like me much and that's why this won't work. If I'm in your life it will drive a wedge between you and Paisley. I can't do that to you or her. She needs her father and you need to be there for her to help her through whatever is bothering her."

"No," Clay breathed. "We can all sit down and work this out," he offered. Abi had offered to do just that tomorrow and he was hopeful that they'd be able to come to some truce that would help heal the rift between Paisley and Rose. He wouldn't give up the woman he loved just because his teenage daughter was being a brat.

"Sitting down with Paisley is a good idea," Rose said. Clay took a deep breath and let it out.

"I'm so glad to hear you say that, Honey," Clay said.

"Paisley needs you and Abi to lay down some rules but she also needs your understanding and unconditional love. If I'm in your life, she'll never believe you are giving her either of those things. Go be with your family." Rose turned to shut the door in his face and he stuck his boot-clad foot in the way.

"You're my family, Rose. Don't shut me out," he begged.

"I'm sorry, Clay. This is for the best, really," she said. Rose looked down to where his boot was still holding her door open and back up at him as if expecting him to just comply.

"This isn't over, Rose. I won't give up on you—on us. I'll let you hide away tonight but I'll be back. I love you," he said and pulled his foot free from her door jam. Rose gently shut the door, closing him out and putting up her walls. He wouldn't let her hide for long though. He meant it when he said he'd be back. He planned on spending every waking minute trying to convince Rose that they are made for each other, even if she couldn't see it for herself right now.

ROSE

Rose spent the better part of a week dodging Clay's calls and pretending not to be in her townhome every morning he came over banging on her door, demanding to talk to her. He had even shown up at the office and she had security show him back out. Corbin and Aiden joked that she was abusing her power and authority as their mom and personal assistant. Maybe they were both right but she didn't care. She wasn't ready to face down Clay yet because if she did, she'd give in to everything he wanted from her. She'd spill her guts and tell him she was in love with him too and that would ruin his relationship with his daughter.

Clay had texted that he and Abi had sat Paisley down and talked with her about what she had done. Rose couldn't blame the girl. She wanted her parents to get back together and thought that if Rose was out of the picture, they'd have the chance of rekindling their marriage. Clay's message said that he and Abi explained that would never happen. They had been divorced for so long now, getting back together wasn't something that either of them wanted.

Besides his recap of his discussion with Paisley and Abi, he had messaged her daily begging her to give him another chance. He told her all the things she so desperately wanted to hear and believe but words weren't enough. Words wouldn't fix his daughter's hating her. That would take time and she wasn't a spring chicken. What she and Clay had was very real but giving in to what they both needed wouldn't fix their problems. She couldn't give him anymore—she just didn't have it in her, even if she was completely in love with him.

Rose hurried into Aiden's office and sat down in front of his big desk. Today was the big day they had all been working so hard for. If everything went well, they'd close the biggest deal their company ever had. Corbin and Aiden were about crazy with all the last minute details and she couldn't get her head out of her ass and stop thinking so much about Clay.

Aiden looked up from the pile of papers he was studying and nodded. "Rose," he said. "Thanks for putting in so much overtime. You know that Corbin and I would be lost without you, right?" She smiled and nodded. He wasn't wrong. Aiden was in his second year of office as a Senator and she knew that he had very little time for the company but he made this project his baby and there was no keeping him away from closing the deal.

"How does Zara feel about you spending so much time at the office?" she asked. Rose knew first-hand that Zara was done with the whole "I have to work late" thing. "And the girls must miss you too," Rose added for good measure.

Aiden looked up at her again and smirked. "You know damn well that my wife isn't very happy with me right now. She hasn't been in for lunch all week. I think it's her way of punishing me." Aiden's famous lunches with his wife usually ended up with them both naked in his locked office and Rose trying to pretend she didn't hear Zara's pleas for Aiden to "not stop". Even Corbin noticed the lack of lunch meetings between Zara and Aiden and her son brought the topic up every chance he got to ride Aiden's ass and piss him off. It was nice the way her two boys loved each other more like brothers than best friends. But, that meant they fought like brothers too and this week, with the tensions riding so high about this deal, there was a whole lot of fighting going on in the office.

"I promised to take her and the girls on a family vacation as soon as this deal is finished and I have to head to Washington, DC for this year's session," Aiden said.

"Oh—that sounds great," Rose said. "Where are you guys going?"

Aiden sighed, "Disney—again. But, I'm hoping that a few days there will make the girls happy and then we can head to our beach house." Aiden had a few homes around the country, as did Corbin. Rose had a little condo on the coast but she didn't see the need for a fancy beach house like the boys had. If she wanted to spend a day at the beach with her grandchildren, she could go to their home and that left her condo as her place to sit back and relax.

"Well, you are married to a saint, so I'm sure she'll agree to your plan," Rose teased. Zara was a wonderful woman and she balanced out Aiden's crazy obsessive need for his life to be perfect. She was his chaos and his sanity all rolled up in one person. Clay was that for Rose and she wasn't sure if she'd ever find another person like him to fill that void in her life. She wasn't expecting to find Clay in the first place. She wasn't looking for anyone but once she found him, he seemed to take over the dark crevices of her heart and made them lighter.

"Yeah—Zara's pretty awesome. Especially for putting up with me and my ambitions." Aiden chuckled at his statement. "How are you doing, Rose?"

"Fine," she lied. "I'm good."

"Liar," Aiden accused. "You raised me not to tell lies, Rose. You think that I can't see what's going on with you. You're the closest thing I've ever had to a mom, Rose. I see that you're upset."

"And, Corbin told you what happened between Clay and me, right?" she questioned.

Aiden cringed and nodded. "Sorry, but your son can't keep his mouth shut. Hell, if you have a secret you don't want anyone else to know, don't tell Corbin." Aiden was right but it still upset her that her son was spreading the news about her and Clay.

"Crap," Rose groaned. "I wanted to keep this all to myself. You know, work through my problems and not drag everyone else down with me." She was always the one helping everyone around her to pick up the pieces when their lives fell apart. She was the mom in the equation between her, Aiden, and Corbin. Having the tables turned felt plain wrong.

"What are you going to do—you know about Clay?" Aiden asked.

Rose sat back on the sofa and kicked off her heels. "I have no idea," she moaned. "I know what I should do but it doesn't add up to what I want to do."

"What do you think you should do here Rose?" Aiden questioned.

"I think I should let him go. My being in Clay's life will only destroy his relationship with his daughter. Do you remember being thirteen, Aiden?" He nodded and smiled. "I can sure remember you boys at that age. You were so impressionable. I'd never let anyone or anything come between the three of us. How can I stay with him knowing that I'd be hurting that poor girl?"

Aiden chuckled, "That poor girl tried to shove you out of Clay's life by sending a fake message to break the two of you up. I think that 'poor girl' as you call her is going to be just fine if you stay a part of Clay's life. Sure, she'll give you a lot of shit because she is a teenager, but don't let her make your decisions for you."

"I get that, I just hate knowing that whatever decision I make, I'm hurting someone," Rose almost whispered.

"Including yourself," Aiden offered. "You're avoiding the most important point in all this."

"What's that?" she asked.

"Do you love him?" Aiden asked. Rose gasped and

covered her mouth to hide her sob. "Oh Rose," Aiden breathed.

"I know," she cried. "I'm pathetic. I do love him and God, that sounds so silly since I've only known him for a couple of months. What am I going to do?" she asked.

Aiden stood and rounded his desk, pulling Rose up from her perch on his sofa and into a bear hug. She smiled and wrapped her arms around him.

"Isn't this supposed to be my job?" she questioned. "You know, comforting you?"

"Sometimes it's all right to let other people take care of you, Rose. I know you don't like us to make a fuss but get over it. I won't pretend to have the answer you need. Don't you think it's time to be happy for yourself? Isn't it about time that you do something for you and stop overthinking everything? Just be happy Rose." Aiden let her go and she wiped at the tears that fell down her face.

"Thanks, Aiden," she said. "Now, I'm going to go to the ladies' room to fix my makeup. You good for the meeting?"

"Yep," he said. "Corbin and I have everything we need. We've got this if you want to knock off a little early," Aiden offered. Rose didn't hide her smile. He knew her too well.

"I would like that," she said. "I think I need to go have a talk with a certain cowboy."

Aiden chuckled, "Good luck," he said.

"You'll tell Corbin for me?" she questioned. Aiden made a face and she giggled.

"Fuck no," he grumbled. "You can do that yourself.

I'm not sure who's going to give you more trouble in all of this—the teenage girl or Corbin."

"Well, crap," Rose mumbled. Aiden laughed again and walked her out of his office. She decided to deal with her son later, sneaking off to the ladies' room before he came out of his office. Sure, she was being a coward but she could only deal with one crisis at a time. First, she needed to find Clay and see if he wanted to hear her out. Then, they would need to sit down and figure out what to do about their kids—one problem at a time.

CLAYTON

Clay was trying to stay busy around the ranch but keeping his mind off Rose was nearly impossible for him to do. She was all he could think about. The question was would he be able to persuade her to give him another chance. He had spent the good part of every day banging on her front door and begging her to just come out and talk to him. He'd gone by her office only to be tossed out on his ear. He was starting to feel that she wasn't ever going to let him back into her life but that wasn't something he could just accept. He needed Rose and sooner or later, she'd come to her senses and realize she needed him just as much.

Clay looked at the foal that had been born just over a week ago and smiled. "What should I do boy?" he asked, patting down the baby's side. The foal whinnied, causing Clay to laugh.

"Yeah, I got it—go talk to her. But, what if Rose doesn't listen?" Clay asked.

"Maybe she's ready to give listening a shot," Rose said, standing in the side doorway to the barn.

"Rose," he said, backing away from the pen he had just mucked out. "You're here," he said. Clay was never one to feel tongue-tied but right now, staring down the woman he loved, he was having a hard time coming up with the right words to say.

"I am," she said, sassy smirk firmly in place. "I'm glad to find you here too."

"I was just finishing up for the night and then I was going to come by your place," he admitted. "To pound on your door and beg you to talk to me."

Rose sighed and looked down at the floor. "I'm sorry about that, Clay. I was being a chicken and well, I didn't want to make the wrong decision. I just needed some time." She had taken a little over a week to come to her senses but Clay wouldn't point that out. Rose was here now and that was all that mattered to him. Well, that and if she was going to give him another chance to prove to her that they were made for each other.

"Did your time help?" he asked.

"Yeah," she agreed. "I think it did."

"Did you come all this way to tell me goodbye again, Rose?" he asked. God, he hated that might be the case but he wanted her to have a voice in their relationship. He knew that was important for Rose. She had given up so much in life he wanted to give her everything. Her submission was a gift but he wouldn't take her decisions from her.

"No," Rose said. "I didn't come here to tell you good-bye, Clay. I came here to tell you that I love you."

Clay pulled the pen door closed and locked it so the foal wouldn't be able to get lose. He was afraid to cross the barn to where Rose stood. He needed to make sure that he had heard her correctly. "Say that again," he demanded.

"I love you," she said. Her smile nearly lit up the entire barn and he didn't hesitate to go to her.

"I love you too, Rose," he said.

She giggled, "I know," she admitted. "I heard you tell Corbin that you loved me when you were at my house last week. So, you still do—love me—that is?"

"I do, Rose. That night, when you left here, I was going to ask you to marry me."

Rose gasped, "I thought you just wanted me to move in with you," she said.

"Well, sure. But that wasn't enough. I didn't want to spook you, so I waited. I just couldn't wait anymore, Rose." Clay stared her down and he felt his damn heart beating like it was going to pound right out of his chest.

"I'm not a horse, Clay. You won't spook me," she said. Clay reached for her and pulled Rose against his body.

"How about you promise not to run off and I promise to try not fucking things up too badly," Clay offered. Rose giggled.

"Not quite how I was going to put it, but deal," she said.

"Good," Clay said. "Then let's get this part over with." He got down on one knee and reached into his coveralls, pulling out the ring box that he had been keeping in his pocket since she left over a week ago.

"Marry me, Rose," he said. "Spend the rest of our lives with me, please." Rose covered her mouth with a shaking hand and gasped.

"Clay," she whispered.

"Is that a yes or a no, Honey?" he asked. He felt like he was holding his damn breath waiting for Rose to give her answer. "Well?"

"Yes," she whispered, nodding and crying. Clay took the ring from its box and slipped it on her finger, not giving her time to change her mind. He stood from the ground and pulled her up into his arms.

"It's official now," he whispered. "You can't change your mind now—I put a ring on it," he teased. He started walking to his house with her in his arms and Rose protested that he needed to put her down, squealing and giggling along the way. Clay swatted her ass, making her yelp.

"Clay," she shouted. "Put me down."

"Not until we get to the playroom," he said.

"O-Oh," Rose breathed. "We're going to play?"

"Yep," he said. "And, I plan on reminding you of all the rules—including the one where you don't run off without talking things through with me."

"That's not one of the rules," Rose challenged.

Clay swatted her ass again and headed down the stairs into the basement of his home. He turned the corner and opened the door to the playroom. "It is now," he said. "You don't like something; you and I talk it through. Otherwise, this thing between us won't work. Got it?" Rose shyly nodded. "I need the words, Honey," he reminded.

"Yes, Clay. I won't run—promise," she agreed. He lowered her down his body, letting her feel every inch of his erection, loving the way she ground herself against him. She was always his little vixen, taking what she wanted from him.

"You are bad," he said, pointing an accusing finger at her.

"You going to punish me, Sir?" she asked.

"Is that what you want, Rose?" he asked. "You want me to punish you for being naughty?"

"Yes, Sir," she breathed, kissing his neck. She gently bit the sensitive skin just under his ear and he swatted her ass.

"Strip and get on the saddle," he ordered. Rose's breath hitched and he gave her fleshy globe another smack, just for good measure.

"You brought it back into the playroom?" she asked.

"Yep, now do as I asked, Rose," he commanded. Rose quickly stripped out of her skirt and blouse, leaving just her thigh highs that made him half-crazy with lust, her skimpy lace thong, and her lacy, see-through bra. God, she was his walking wet dream.

"Fuck, Baby," he whispered. "Stop there. Leave all that on and keep the heels," he ordered. She nodded and reached for his hand so he could help her up onto the saddle. Rose leaned forward, gifting him with the sight of her perfect ass perched and ready for his attention.

"Like this, Sir?" she taunted. Rose knew exactly how he wanted her and she also knew what her submission did to him. He needed a minute to get his unruly cock under control.

"Yeah," he said. "Just like that, Baby." He smacked her ass, leaving a red mark where his hand had landed. "Flogger or paddle tonight?" he asked. "I'll leave that decision to you."

"Whichever you want, Sir," Rose said. Clay knew she liked the paddle, so he reached for it, and Rose gifted him with her sexy smile as she watched him over her shoulder.

"I take it you approve?" he asked, holding up the paddle for her to inspect.

"Yes, Sir," she admitted. "I love it when you use the paddle on me."

"Thank you for telling me that, Honey." Clay loved the way Rose had learned to share her likes and dislikes with him. It was an important part of their give and take as Dom and sub.

"I'm going to go to twenty-five and I want for you to count for me, Rose," he ordered.

"Yes, Sir," she stuttered. His Rose always was up for a challenge. He rubbed her ass and gave the right cheek the first smack with the paddle. She hissed out her breath and he waited for her to count for him.

"One," she yelped.

He landed a hard whack on the left cheek and she cried out. "Two," she shouted.

He kept going, rubbing his big hand over her flesh in between blows, to help her ride out the pain. When he got to twelve, Clay dipped two fingers through her wet folds and loved the way she moaned and pushed back against his hand, as if insisting he give her more.

"You love to play, don't you, Honey?" he asked.

"Yes," Clay she hissed. "I need more," she said. "Please, Sir."

"I'll take good care of you, Honey," Clay promised. He withdrew his fingers from her drenched pussy and she mewled her protest, causing him to chuckle. He gave her already welted, red ass another smack and she cried out and moaned. Rose kept count and he watched her, so proud of his sub. When he got to twenty-five, Clay dropped the paddle to the tile floor and undid his jeans. His cock was screaming for attention and he could see Rose's arousal coating her thighs. She was more than ready to take him and he wanted to get into her pussy more than he wanted his next breath.

"This is going to be hard and fast, Honey," he said. Clay pulled her from the saddle and she cuddled against his body. He carried her over to the leather couch he had in the corner of his playroom and laid her down. Rose hissed when her hot flesh hit the cold leather and he wasted no time. Clay drug her body to the edge of the sofa and plunged balls deep inside of her.

"You feel so fucking good," he groaned. He stilled, getting himself under control. He promised her hard and fast and he wanted to deliver on both counts, not just the fast part. Clay pumped in and out of her body, loving the breathy little moans he elicited from her parted lips. He dipped down to kiss his way into her mouth, letting his tongue playfully meet her own. She wrapped her arms around his neck, demanding more, and Clay could tell that she was close to finding her orgasm.

He snaked his hand down her body and found her

clit, giving it a playful tap. Rose moaned into his mouth and when he let the pad of his thumb stroke over her sensitive nub, she lost control, riding his cock like the wild force he had come to love. His Rose, his life, his sub. Her pussy milked his cock with the spasms as she rode out her orgasm. He couldn't help but lose himself inside of her, quickly finding his release.

"I'm so glad you bought me a drink on our birthday," Rose whispered.

"I'm so glad you agreed to come home with me, despite your very long list of dating do's and don'ts," Clay said.

"Well, you showed me that there is more to life than living by the rules, Clayton Nash," Rose teased.

"Naw," he drawled. "I just introduced you to a whole new set of rules, my little sub." Rose giggled and they tumbled down onto the sofa together, wrapped up in each other's bodies. Clay wasn't sure how he had gotten so lucky finding her. Rose was the perfect woman for him. The partner he never thought he'd find. The woman he was going to spend the rest of his life with— his cougar submissive.

TYLER

Tyler Nash walked into the bank and the very last thing he wanted to do was beg but that's what he was reduced too. He was going to have to beg for a fucking loan to keep his business afloat. He had always dreamed of owning his own ranch but he wouldn't take the money from his older brother, Clay. He'd offered time and again but that wasn't how he wanted to start things off. No, begging some bank manager who knew nothing about him to give him the cash he needed to buy the land adjacent to his brother's ranch, was so much more reasonable.

He knew that with no collateral and no real money to put up for the down payment, they'd be turning him down flat. But Ty was hoping that his lucky plaid shirt and shined up cowboy boots would sell his whole, "I'm a rancher" vibe.

He walked into the lobby and removed his cowboy hat and got in line to ask for the manager. He waited for his turn with the only teller on duty and when he finally got up to the counter, she put her "This window closed," sign up.

"You're kidding me," he whispered under his breath. "Will someone else be coming to take your place?" he called after the teller. She merely shrugged and walked to the backroom, closing the door between them. "Great, just great," he mumbled.

"I'm so sorry, Sir," a woman's voice called from the back corner. "We're short-staffed today and it's Candy's break. I can help you back here, in my office," she offered. Clay turned to find the sexy redhead standing back in the doorway to her very small office. The walls were all glass, reminding him of a fishbowl.

"Thanks," he said, walking back to her office. "I appreciate that. I'm inquiring about a business loan and I'd like to speak with a manager."

"Well, then it's your lucky day," the woman said. She waved him into her office and pointed to one of the very uncomfortable looking chairs that sat in front of her desk. He waited for her to round her desk and find her chair before sitting. It was ingrained in him to be a gentleman and sitting before a lady was something his Mama would have boxed his ears for.

"What can I do for you, Mr.—" She held out her hand to him and waited for him to take it.

"Tyler Nash but you can call me Ty," he offered.

"It's good to meet you, Mr. Nash," she said, stressing his last name. He smiled and nodded. "I'm Lucinda Dixon, this branch's manager. I think I can help you with your request." Ty wanted to laugh at how proper Lucinda Dixon was but he dug the whole business vibe she was giving off. She had on a tailored gray pinstripe business pantsuit that hugged her every curve. The blazer was covering up an almost see-through white blouse that had just the right number of buttons undone to make his mouth water. He didn't miss her heels that made him just about lose his mind when he watched her cross her legs and swing her foot around playfully. Ty needed to get his head on straight because that wasn't why he was there today. No, he needed to get pretty little Lucinda Dixon to give him a loan.

"Now, what kind of business are you needing the loan for Mr. Nash?" she asked, getting right down to it.

"Right," he said, clearing his throat. "You're not much into small talk, are you Lucy?" he questioned.

She shot him a look that told him she wasn't. "My name is Lucinda and I'd prefer you call me Ms. Dixon," she said.

Ty chuckled, "All right, sorry," he said. "You know, you look very familiar, Ms. Dixon," he said. She looked him over, her eyes flaring when they reached his again and he knew he was onto something. She knew him, that much was clear. Hell, everyone seemed to know everyone else in their small town. She looked to be a few years younger than him but if he had to guess, she remembered him from high school or something.

"Were you in my class?" he asked. Lucinda put her pen down and looked across her desk at him.

"No," she breathed.

"Right, you are a lot younger than I am, sorry," he offered.

"Not that much younger," she challenged.

"So, we didn't graduate together but were we at Milford High at the same time?" he asked. She shyly looked down at her laptop and fiddled with some papers on her desk. Ty tried to think back to his high school years, trying to remember a red-headed beauty and drew a blank. "Did you always have red hair?"

"Yes," she murmured. "If you don't mind, I have a very busy day. Can we continue with your application?"

He wanted to tell her no but he needed this loan to buy the land before someone else snatched it up. "All right," he agreed. "You know we could speed this up if you just tell me how we know each other."

Lucinda picked up her pen and cleared her throat. "How about you tell me what you plan on using the loan for?"

"Sure," Ty said. "I want to buy land for a ranch."

"I thought that you and Clay ran Lowdown Ranch together?" she asked.

"Now see, you do know me," Ty said, wagging his finger at her accusingly.

Lucinda shrugged and looked back at her laptop. "So, you'll be starting a new business venture aside from the ranch you run with your brother?"

"It will be a separate entity," he agreed. "Did you go to school with my brother?"

"No," she almost shouted. "He's like ten years older than me. Although he was friends with my older brother."

"So, you have a brother that went to school with Clay?" Ty pushed.

"No," she said. "My brother went to school with you.

You both graduated from Milford the same year." Now he was getting somewhere. Not knowing how the hell he knew Lucinda was starting to piss him off.

"Wait—your brother is Ford Dixon?" He remembered Ford, they played on the football team together.

"Yes," she said through her clenched teeth. Ty could tell that she wasn't very happy about his questions. "Can we please get on with this?"

"Sure, sorry," he said. "I didn't mean to upset you, Ms. Dixon."

"It's fine," she lied. "I'd just rather not talk about my personal life while at work. If you are here on business, I'd like to get on with it."

"Sounds good, Ms. Dixon. Next question," he prompted. Lucinda studied her computer screen and chewed on the tip of her pen. The whole scene made him hot but he was pretty sure that saying so wouldn't be considered business-like and the last thing he wanted was to piss Lucinda off enough to get him thrown out of her office.

She cleared her throat, "Will you have a co-signer on the loan?" she asked.

"No," he said.

"Not even your brother?" she asked.

"No," he said.

"How about a spouse or girlfriend?" she questioned.

"Is a co-signer necessary?" he asked.

"Um, no," she squeaked. "It just makes things easier sometimes. We can move on from that question." Ty nodded. A part of him wanted to tell her that he had no wife or significant other but that would be crossing the whole business/personal border she had put up. He'd stick with the facts and his relationship status wasn't her business or a fact that she needed to know. But, why did he want to tell her those personal details more than he wanted to do just about anything else?

LUCINDA

Lucy pushed long strands of hair back from her face and tucked them back into the messy bun she usually wore for work. She was so self-conscious about the way Ty Nash was watching her. When she was just a teenager, she would have given just about anything to have him looking at her like he was now. But, he was a high school golden boy who didn't give her a second thought when they passed in the hallways day after day. Lucy was two years behind him and her brother, Ford, in high school and God, she had such a crush on him. Every girl did. He was the quarterback on the football team and girls followed him around like lovesick puppies, her included.

She pushed her glasses up the bridge of her nose, noting the way Tyler's eyes seemed to follow her every movement. Lucy knew he was only studying her to figure out how they knew each other but it still made her hot and somewhat bothered. His blue eyes were always so intense and having them on her now made her girly parts do a happy dance. No—he was just here for a loan, nothing else.

"How much are you looking to borrow, Mr. Nash?" she asked. She had stopped herself from calling him Ty a few times now. She knew that everyone called him that but she just couldn't. How many nights had she dreamed of calling him by his nickname while he was holding her in his arms? How many times did she imagine screaming out his name when she got herself off thinking about him? Yeah—it would be one colossal fucking bad idea to call him Ty.

"The land is valued at two-hundred and five thousand but I think I can get it a little lower than that price," he said. "Plus, I'll need to build a barn or two and the main house. All in, I'm thinking five-hundred thousand should do it."

Lucy stopped typing and looked over her laptop at him. He was sitting back in one of the two crappy chairs she had in her little office, ankle resting over his leg like he just hadn't asked her to approve his half-million-dollar loan. He smiled at her and even dared to wink. Lucy rolled her eyes and looked back down at her screen.

"That's an awfully big ask, Mr. Nash. You have any collateral?" She already asked if he had a co-signer, although that was more of a fishing expedition on her part, to find out if he had a wife or girlfriend. Not that it mattered.

"No," he breathed. "Listen," Ty sat forward on his seat, firmly planting both feet on the floor in front of himself. "I've been in ranching my whole life. When our dad died, my brother and I took over his ranch and we've been partners since. Ranching is in my blood and I just know that this property will be perfect for raising cattle. It's been a part of the Phillip's place and now, they are auctioning the land off to the highest bidder. I want to be the person it goes to but I can't do that without a loan."

She was mesmerized at how passionate he seemed about his work. It made Lucy wonder how passionate he might be about other things he loved in his life. That was a rabbit hole she couldn't go down though. Professional—she needed to remember to be completely professional in this little meeting otherwise, she'd be stamping "approved" on his loan and that would end up getting her fired.

"Do you have anything to put down on the loan?" she asked again.

"I have a small nest egg, but it isn't much—only about twenty-thousand."

"Well, that's at least a start," she said. "Let me get the rest of your personal information and I will see what I can do. It's a large loan, so I will need to run it past my boss before I can make a final decision."

Tyler stood and nodded, "Does that mean you'll consider it, Lucy?"

"Ms. Dixon," she reminded. "And, yes. But, don't get your hopes up. I'm not sure our little bank can float such a large sum of money."

"Okay," he breathed. "Let's give it a try. What do you need to know about me?"

Everything. "Oh, you know just the usual stuff—date

of birth, social security number, address, and relationship status." She wanted to kick herself for slipping that one in. Sure, she would have to put if he was married or single on the form, but it wasn't something she wanted to make a big deal out of.

Ty smiled and sat back down in his seat. "Single," he said. "How about you?"

"Um, my relationship status isn't something we need to fill out on your loan papers, Mr. Nash," she protested. Although, it felt good to have him showing interest in her. She needed to remember that Tyler Nash was a flirt and someone she should steer clear of if she wanted to keep her heart in one piece.

"Come on now, Lucy. Turnabout is fair play. I'll show you mine if you show me yours," Ty teased. God, she wanted to tell him she'd show him anything he wanted to see but that wouldn't be professional at all. "How about we start with an easier question," he offered.

She wanted to tell him no and ask him the next question on the loan application but she found herself nodding her agreement like a lunatic. Lucy inwardly chastised herself for being such a fool. "Great," he said, sexy smirk firmly in place. "Will you go out with me on a date?" he asked.

"A date," she squeaked, sure she hadn't heard him correctly.

"Yeah—you know, dinner or a movie. Hell, how about both," he said.

"I don't think that's a good idea," she whispered. "You are applying for a loan at my bank."

"All right, to make it fair, how about you work on the loan and get back to me with your answer. Then, we can circle back to my question," he said.

"And, if I deny your loan?" she asked. "You'll still want to go out on a date with me?" She was holding her breath, waiting for him to answer and when he smiled and nodded, she couldn't help but smile. Tyler Nash was asking her out on a date and even though her mind was shouting at her that it was a fucking awful idea, her heart was doing a little butterfly dance in her damn chest.

"It's just a date, Lucy," he said. "Say yes."

"Yes," she whispered. "I'll go on a date with you."

The End

Owned Book 4- His Nerdy Submissive coming soon!

ABOUT K.L. RAMSEY

Romance Rebel fighting for Happily Ever After!

K. L. Ramsey currently resides in West Virginia (Go Mountaineers!). In her spare time, she likes to read romance novels, go to WVU football games and attend book club (aka-drink wine) with girlfriends.
K. L. enjoys writing Contemporary Romance, Erotic Romance, and Sexy Ménage! She loves to write strong, capable women and bossy, hot as hell alphas, who fall ass over tea kettle for them. And of course, her stories always have a happy ending.

ABOUT K.L. RAMSEY

K.L. Ramsey's social media links:
Facebook-> https://www.facebook.com/kl.ramsey.58
(OR) https://www.facebook.com/k.l.ramseyauthor/
Twitter-> https://twitter.com/KLRamsey5
Instagram -> https://www.instagram.com/itsprivate2/
Pinterest-> https://www.pinterest.com/klramsey6234/
Goodreads-> https://www.goodreads.com/author/
show/17733274.K_L_Ramsey
Book Bub-> https://www.bookbub.com/profile/k-l-
ramsey Amazon.com-> https://www.amazon.com/K.
L.-Ramsey/e/B0799P6JGJ/
Ramsey's Rebels-> https://www.facebook.com/
groups/ramseysrebels/
Website-> https://klramsey.wixsite.com/mysite
KL Ramsey & BE Kelly's ARC Team->
https://www.facebook.com/
groups/klramseyandbekellyarcteam
KL Ramsey & BE Kelly's Street Team->
https://www.facebook.com/
groups/klramseyandbekellystreetteam
Newsletter->https://mailchi.mp/
4e73ed1b04b9/authorklramsey

BE Kelly's social media links:

Instagram-> https://www.
instagram.com/bekellyparanormalromanceauthor/
Facebook-> https://www.facebook.com/be.kelly.564
Twitter-> https://twitter.com/BEKelly9
Book bub-> https://www.bookbub.com/profile/be-kelly
Amazon->https://www.amazon.com/BE-Kelly/e/B081LLD38M
BE Kelly's Reader's group-> https://www.facebook.com/groups/530529814459269/

MORE WORKS BY K.L. RAMSEY

The Relinquished Series Box Set (Coming soon)
Love Times Infinity
Love's Patient Journey
Love's Design
Love's Promise

Harvest Ridge Series Box Set (Coming soon)
Worth the Wait
The Christmas Wedding
Line of Fire
Torn Devotion
Fighting for Justice

Last First Kiss Series Box Set (Coming soon)
Theirs to Keep
Theirs to Love
Theirs to Have
Theirs to Take

Second Chance Summer Series
True North
The Wrong Mr. Right

Ties That Bind Series
Saving Valentine
Blurred Lines
Dirty Little Secrets

Taken Series
Double Bossed
Double Crossed

Owned
His Secret Submissive
His Reluctant Submissive
His Cougar Submissive

Royal Bastards MC
Savage Heat
Whiskey Tango (Coming Soon)

Savage Hell MC Series
RoadKill
REPOssession (Coming soon)

Alphas in Uniform
Hellfire
Destiny (Coming soon)

Works by BE Kelly (K.L.'s alter ego…)

Reckoning MC Seer Series
Reaper
Tank
Raven

Perdition MC Shifter Series
Ringer
Rios
Trace (Coming soon)
Gray (Coming soon)